ARMAND V.

DAG SOLSTAD

Armand V.

Footnotes to an Unexcavated Novel

translated by Steven T. Murray

A NEW DIRECTIONS BOOK

This translation has been published with the financial support of NORLA, Norwegian Literature Abroad.

Manufactured in the United States of America
New Directions Books are printed on acid-free paper
First published in 2018 as New Directions Paperbook 1418

Library of Congress Cataloging-in-Publication Data
Names: Solstad, Dag, 1941– author. | Murray, Steven T., translator.
Title: Armand V. : footnotes to an unexcavated novel / by Dag Solstad ; translated by Steven T. Murray.
Description: First edition. | New York : New Directions Publishing Corporation, 2018. | "A New Directions Book." | First published in Norwegian as Armand V. : fotnoter til en uutgravd roman.
Identifiers: LCCN 2018002147 (print) | LCCN 2018013556 (ebook) | ISBN 9780811226295 () | ISBN 9780811226288 (alk. paper)
Subjects: LCSH: Diplomats—Fiction. | Fathers and sons—Fiction. | Choice (Psychology)—Fiction. | Life change events—Fiction. | Norway—Fiction. | Middle East—Fiction. | Psychological fiction.
Classification: LCC PT8951.29.O5 (ebook) | LCC PT8951.29.O5 A7613 2018 (print) | DDC 839.823/74—dc23
LC record available at https://lccn.loc.gov/2018002147

10 9 8 7 6 5 4 3 2 1

New Directions Books are published for James Laughlin
by New Directions Publishing Corporation
80 Eighth Avenue, New York 10011

ARMAND V.

1. This footnote, the very first, suffers from having a displaced time perspective. It originates from a specific event that has to do with Armand's youth; however, it does not deal with Armand's youth but with his son's youth, as viewed by Armand, a man in his sixties. This footnote is a commentary on something that took place in a completely different time, and at a completely different place, and with characters who are altogether different, such as Armand, or those who aren't even included here in this text at this time (such as Armand's son, who wasn't born yet); this was a time almost twenty years before Armand would meet the woman who'd later become his son's mother, and yet the son is a central figure in this footnote, in this scene that illuminates his father's youth.

1 B. One morning not so long ago Armand awoke and decided that he had to visit his son, whom he had not seen in well over half a year. He was wide awake when he made this decision, but immediately prior, he had been wrapped in a doze, from which this clear thought had sprung. Half a year ago, when it was winter in Oslo, his son had lived with him for a while because

Armand was about to go on a lengthy trip abroad, and it had seemed fitting that his son, who lived in a little room half an hour's walk from Armand's apartment, should move in and look after this spacious apartment, while he, the father, was away. The son moved in with him three or four days before his departure, and lay sleeping in the guest room when Armand left the apartment on a dark winter morning to begin his extended trip abroad by taking a taxi out to Oslo International Airport, which was located at Gardermoen in the Norwegian interior, not far from Lake Mjøsa. From there he took an early morning flight to a city in central Europe, where he immediately commenced the business which was the purpose of his trip abroad. For week after week he flitted around Europe, by plane or train, until he eventually arrived in one of the absolute largest European metropolises, the last stop on his long foreign sojourn, where he had booked a hotel room for five days. However, he left this city the very next morning, because an appointment he was supposed to have that day had been canceled, and since he had also begun to suffer from what was for him a surprising but acute sense of boredom from traveling abroad, especially staying in this metropolis, which he had found so pleasant to visit previously, and which he had looked forward to seeing again with his own eyes, wanting to wander through the streets that were so enticing, he decided, at the instant the cancellation of the appointment was confirmed and he had hung up the phone, to pack his bags, take the elevator down to the lobby, pay the bill for his stay, and then take a taxi out to the airport, where at the Scandinavian Airlines counter he could exchange his ticket for the next flight to Oslo; there were seats available, because the business that had prompted this trip abroad was such that he had been issued tickets which could easily be altered. He arrived home the same day, his plane having landed at Gardermoen in the late afternoon.

At 6:30 in the evening he unlocked the door to his apartment. It was still wintertime, and snow was coming down. Wet snow, which had settled white on the shoulders of his coat, and which would soon melt as he stood there in the entryway about to hang up his coat on a hook. He heard voices in the apartment, not only his son's, but also a woman's. He set down his bags and took a few steps forward, toward the door that stood half-open into the living room. But then he stopped short. Through the half-open door he saw a terrible scene. A young man, wearing only underpants, was kneeling before a young, fully dressed woman. A young humiliation. His own son was being debased by a young woman, a girl. The girl tossed her head, and her hair swung softly around her; she gave him such a look of contempt, while his son trembled in his abject state. Armand tiptoed in shock into his own bedroom across the hall and closed the door carefully behind him so as not to make the slightest sound. Once inside he stood there ramrod straight in his winter coat, which he had not yet bothered to take off, and with the snow melting on the shoulders. He was rigid with horror.

He remained standing like that until he eventually heard the young woman come out in the hall with hurried footsteps, pausing a moment, probably to put on her coat, before the front door slammed after her, but he also waited until he ascertained that his son, as expected, hadn't left the apartment with her, but was still there. Because after a long while he heard hesitant,

5

indistinct footsteps out in the hall, back and forth, until they faded away again, but without any door being closed and locked; on the contrary, his son must have moved in the other direction, his footsteps indistinct, toward the kitchen, and when Armand realized this, he remained standing as if petrified, his back still ramrod straight, wearing his winter coat in his own bedroom, behind his closed door. He was shaken. Such humiliation. His half-naked son on his knees in front of a woman, debased. It was impossible to erase. Forever. The image was bloody and true. He didn't know what to do about it. Bloody. True. The blood flowed, in the worst way imaginable, the worst conceivable, it was as if he waded in it where he stood. He had to get away. His son's indistinct footsteps returned, now he was going into the living room. As long as his son was in the living room, Armand could not sneak out to the hall, drag his suitcases into the stairwell, and disappear. He sat down on the edge of the bed, still wearing his winter coat. He had to escape from this situation, but how? He got up, went over to the door, and listened. Not a sound. Where was his son? Was he still in the living room? He'd be able to hear Armand if he went out in the hall and left the apartment. And his suitcases would still be there after he left. Had his son already seen them? If so, why hadn't he checked to see if his father was in the bedroom? The humiliating scene was awash in blood. He had to stay here until he heard his son's footsteps again, and he listened again and again to where they took him, until he was utterly certain that they took him, his son, out to the kitchen, and he, Armand, could slip away unnoticed. Finally this happened, and the father, who had long since removed his heavy winter shoes, picked them up and quickly sneaked into the hall, over to the front door, opened it, and then closed it silently, carefully turning the key in the Yale lock.

Then Armand went to a restaurant and ate a decent dinner, with a good bottle of red wine, followed by coffee and cognac. A little after midnight he let himself back into the apartment, which was completely dark. His son had either gone to bed or gone out. Armand hung up his winter coat, changed his shoes, took his suitcases into the bedroom, and unpacked, putting his clothes away in drawers and on shelves, as well as setting all his papers, etc., on a table. Then he went into the bathroom and got ready for bed.

In the morning he met his son, who had just gotten up and who was, or acted like he was, surprised to see him back home. Armand explained that he had returned the night before because an appointment had been canceled. His son nodded, saying that it was time he moved back to his own place. His father summoned all his inner strength, his utmost internal reserves, to say in a calm voice that there was no hurry, but his son shrugged and said that he'd had the apartment at his disposal for over a month now, and it was high time he returned to his normal routines. He went into the bedroom he'd been using, and in an amazingly short time he packed and came out with his two bags and said goodbye to his father.

After that Armand didn't see his son for well over six months, until one morning he woke up and decided that today he would visit him. But the sight he had witnessed in the living room had not faded from his mind. It was just as clear, or unclear, as the day he saw it. He was unable to reconstruct the scene in detail, since he hadn't seen it clearly. He had seen the young woman, the girl, who had debased his half-naked son. He had not seen anything more, or he was unable to say he had. If he tried, he froze up and turned mute. He wasn't even able to describe the way in which she had debased his son, except that he was half-naked and kneeling in front of her, wearing only his underpants, while she was fully dressed. Armand tried to shake off the scene by not thinking about his son over the following weeks and months, except in brief, nagging moments, which in itself was not so remarkable, since his son had long since turned twenty years old and had to be regarded as independent both financially and otherwise. And so he hadn't worried that his son did not contact him.

Now it was obvious to Armand that he wanted to visit his son today. Before noon he left his apartment to take the half-hour walk to where his son lived in a rented room in an apartment building from the 1930s above the Majorstua district, in the direction of Fagerborg. Actually he had something else to do that morning, but he phoned and postponed his plans till the next day. Although, he thought, I should have done the opposite and kept my original appointments, visiting my son tomorrow instead, or early this evening. His son was a student, and he was more likely to find him home in the late afternoon or early evening than in the morning when students were often in the university's reading rooms or attending seminars. If he's not at home in his room then he's not, but I'd better try to visit him now that I've already postponed today's appointments, Armand thought. He'd left his apartment in Skillebekk and walked up Frederik Stangs Gate toward Bygdøy Allé and on toward Frognerveien, which he crossed to continue up toward

Briskeby; then turning up to Majorstua and Bogstadveien, where he crossed before he came to the building where his son rented a room in the apartment of an elderly woman. She rented out two rooms because she had only a meager pension, and in one lived his son; Armand didn't think he had anything in particular to do with the young man who rented the other room, also a student. But he could be mistaken, because he based his assumptions only on the fact that his son hadn't mentioned this other student when he had visited his father or had dinner with him at a restaurant, and on the fact that he never saw the student or heard him mentioned when he, Armand, visited his son in his room. Armand had reached the end of Løvenskiolds Gate, up in Briskeby, where the fire station loomed at the top of the hill and where the former transformer station, which had been converted to a restaurant, especially popular among successful young people, was situated on the left-hand side of the street. He then realized that he'd been rather optimistic when he assumed that it was only half an hour's walk from his apartment in Skillebekk to his son's room, because now he'd already been walking for twenty minutes and he'd only reached the halfway point. It takes at least forty minutes, he thought, not thirty as he'd assumed. That was because he'd usually driven over there on his previous visits, and the times he'd walked there he had started from a completely different location than his apartment. Well, well, Armand thought as he started walking up Industrigata, though without picking up his pace, because his pace was brisk enough as it was. I'll get there when I get there, he thought, what makes me think there's any hurry, he might not even be home, in fact it's not certain he'll

9

be there at all. Armand was quite a fit man in his sixties, slim, as he had been his whole life, and he walked with a firm stride up Industrigata. It was a day during the transition between summer and fall, a late-summer day with delicate but clear glimpses of early autumn, such as in the rustling of the leaves. If anyone had asked him he would have confirmed that he thought he'd had a good life till now, and he wouldn't have said so just because he realized it would be extraordinarily unfair to claim the opposite, taking into account the circumstances and the outer signs of success so strongly evident in his appearance. But just as resolutely he attempted to quell a powerful internal scream, seeking to dull the memory, the sight, that had prompted it. That's what he had seen. It was this vision, which had caught up with him, now in the image of his own son. Seeing his son in such a state. Anyone who had seen his own son in that state would have acknowledged this vision. Even though he didn't recognize himself in his son's figure, except as unidentifiable remnants of something, and barely even that, nevertheless he knew that this was a repeated vision of something he had so inadvertently witnessed on that evening six months before.

He was approaching the building where his son rented his room from the elderly woman. The closer he got, the more impatient he became to see his son again face-to-face, though he still thought it was highly unlikely that he would be home at this time of day. He stood at the street door and sought out the landlady's doorbell. He rang the specified number of times to signal a visitor for his son. Two short rings. Visitors to the widow had to press the doorbell for one long ring, and if that didn't work, pause and try again. The signal for visitors to the other lodger was three short rings. Armand pushed the bell for two short rings, and he actually got a response when the street door buzzed and he pushed it open. The apartment was on the third floor, and when he got up there he rang two more times at the apartment door. He heard footsteps in the entry hall, and the door opened. There stood his son. He was dressed in a military uniform and greeted his father with an embarrassed smile.

1 c. His son must have had the embarrassed smile because he hadn't told his father that he was no longer a student, but was now a soldier. He invited Armand into his room, and there he spent a long time apologizing. It had come upon him so suddenly, and there were so many things that had to be arranged.

"Yes, I don't doubt that for a moment," said his father, "because not only did you forget to inform me, but you obviously haven't had time to give notice to your landlady either, or did you intend to keep the room?"

His son said that's exactly what he was now wondering. He'd actually intended to give it up, that was what he'd considered doing during this leave, which was also his first, and his father had been fortunate to catch him now, because he was just here to pack before he returned to base. But then he'd changed his mind. Because otherwise where would he live during his leaves?

"With your mother," replied his father, "or with me."

"I certainly don't want to stay in my old room at Mom's place," said the son.

His father could have said: "What about with me then?" but he just couldn't. Instead he sighed and said that he would pay the rent for his poor soldier of a son. By this time he'd been sitting in his son's room on a kitchen chair watching him finish packing for his return to the base. It's not true that he'd suspected everything would be fine. But he hadn't expected this, and he had no idea what to make of it.

———

2. Oslo also had a lot more to offer even in the 1960s, especially for an ambitious young man. Naturally the text now makes quite an amusing point here, drawing a circle from the Humanities building at the university at Blindern and the building of the Norwegian Broadcasting System in Marienlyst, marked with the southern point of the compass (called the Point of Hope), and then continuing to a point on the radius precisely at the Blindernveien stop on the Sognsvann tram line, moving on in a straight line through the circle, then down again to Gyldendal Norsk Publishers, in order to demarcate the geometrical pattern for the ambitious young students of today. But Armand's life was so much more. It included excursions to a different Oslo, that strange capital with its distinctive, completely anonymous (now vanished) neighborhoods. One of them he used to visit several times a week, when he had left the reading room at Blindern early in the evening and hurried down Kirkeveien to grab a beer downtown, which began out by Majorstua. There was often a whole flock of students rushing down Kirkeveien, storming at last into one of the many cafés located around the central tram stop at Majorstua (where trams from the whole city started and terminated). At ground level was the Majorstua Building with its subway station. Viewed from the hazy distance of memory this flock of students rushing down Kirkeveien re-

minded him of free birds on a wild flight toward a longed-for warmer country.

But this was not Majorstua and its central tram stop, with all the brown-painted cafés back then that were the essence of the other Oslo, the vanished and anonymous Oslo. This was a stretch of road that the flock of students used to hurry along, oblivious of their surroundings, and now forty years later it stuck in Armand's mind as the most peculiar big-city street he knew, and his heart beat faster thinking of the joy he'd felt, together with his fellow students, when they rushed along a big-city street like Kirkeveien, which it undoubtedly was for him, the kid fresh from the provinces. That big-city feeling on this anonymous stretch of road between Suhms Gate and the central interchange at Majorstua was exclusively due to the car traffic and the street lighting that hung on wires over the street. Besides being a big-city street, Kirkeveien is also one of the main arteries leading into Oslo and heavily traveled. The big-city feeling is entirely due to the noise of the passing cars; the steady rhythm would be abruptly broken off, back then as now, whenever he had to stop at a crosswalk as the light was flashing red, and this red flashing could be seen from far off, like an eye. Back then, a construction site on both sides of Kirkeveien between Suhms Gate and Majorstua was anonymous and might seem abandoned. The sidewalks on both sides would be almost deserted except for small flocks of students hurrying down toward Majorstua every now and then.

Later in life, after Armand had long since taken his exams and left the university, he would often come driving up or down Kirkeveien in his car. It may have been in the seventies, eighties, nineties, or at the start of the present century, no matter whether he was living in Norway (in Oslo) or was stationed abroad. Mostly after he was once again living at home, and he always had his own car parked outside. On occasion, like every other driver in the city, he would come driving up or down Kirkeveien. He would again pass that long-gone stretch between Suhms Gate and the Majorstua intersection, but he never paid it any mind, never even glanced at the apartment buildings lining both sides of the road. He naturally concentrated on the traffic light at the intersection of Suhms Gate, and whether he would make it through before it changed from green to red.

But lately he had renewed his familiarity with this vanished neighborhood of the capital. Once a month he would stroll along Kirkeveien, taking the sidewalk along the right side, between the Majorstua intersection and Suhms Gate—the detour to his son's place, as he called it. Once a month he visited the apartment building where his son rented a room and was let in to the apartment by the old landlady, paying her the rent for his son who had now become a soldier. The old widow preferred that the rent be paid in person, and not through the bank, because then she could receive the rent in cash and sign the son's rent book that his father would hand to her after paying the required amount. Then Armand would take his leave, after first casting a glance at the closed door of his son's room, and after listening to hear whether there was any noise coming from inside. He always paid on the first of each month unless it fell on a weekend, when he would pay on the last Friday of the previous month, because he didn't think it fitting to pay the rent to the old widow on weekends. Even though he wouldn't run into his son, whom he figured would be on leave on the weekends, he harbored a small hope of seeing him on a Friday, if he visited the old woman on a Friday afternoon when the first of the month fell on a Saturday or Sunday. If it fell on a Monday, he made sure to bring the rent payment to her early in the morning, in the faint hope that his son would head back to base from his weekend leave sometime on Monday, and maybe he hadn't left his room yet—so far this had never happened.

Armand had a job that made it possible for him to take care of personal errands during what were considered normal working hours as long as he adhered to the agreements and obligations he had signed on to when he took the job. For the past year he'd been walking a lot, or combining riding the tram with walking whenever he had to go somewhere instead of taking his car; this was also true when he had errands to run other than stopping to drop off his son's monthly rent for the old landlady. If he left from his office building he would take the subway from the National Theater station to Majorstua and walk from there to his son's rented room. He would cross the Majorstua intersection until he reached the Thune goldsmith shop, then walk up the right side of Kirkeveien toward the stoplight at Suhms Gate. Then he would head into this now unfamiliar and long-gone neighborhood of the capital which still triggered such clear memories from the time when he was a university student, and where he now proceeded up to Suhms Gate, while as a student he had walked in the opposite direction, on the other side of Kirkeveien, most often with others, preferably in the midst of a flock of students hurrying along, and he, like they, would glance over to the other side of Kirkeveien, where he was walking right now along the almost deserted sidewalk, past the cheap imitations of big-city streets. When he reached the stoplight at Suhms Gate he turned right, though he could have turned in that direction long before and followed Hammerstads Gate almost straight to the apartment building where his son rented a room, but he chose every time to walk up to the stoplight at Suhms Gate and then turn right, going all the way to Schultz' Gate and then back down to the area where his son's rented room was located, a considerable detour. This right side of Kirkeveien, from the Majorstua intersection to the stoplight at Suhms Gate, had changed a good deal over all these years, not because of how the buildings and sidewalks looked, but the general appearance of the neighborhood and shops, and what was supposed to attract people to this part of town, had changed a great deal, although Armand retained a clear perception that everything corresponded to his own sense of time now, let's say in 2005, as it did in 1965, or a little later. So Armand started with the elegant Thune goldsmith shop, one of the most renowned, which had a branch on this busy corner, where he stopped to admire the jewelry in the window, displayed in the familiar continental manner, each in its own etui, which emphasized that each piece was of such unique character that it must be allowed plenty of space in order to do it justice, even if it was merely a small pearl. But what a pearl! And from this exquisite pearl Armand moved up the right side of Kirkeveien and into one of the most anonymous stretches in downtown Oslo. It is so anonymous that it takes a long time before you realize that that's exactly what it is. First Pearls & Diamonds Forever, then McDonald's, and after that the Majorstua post office, before you pass Ole Vigs Gate, and eventually get an idea of what sort of neighborhood you've wandered into. Pearls & Diamonds, McDonald's, and the Majorstua post office are only the bait—bait targeting vastly different mental states and moods, along with different ages and buying power. Armand, for instance, undoubtedly prefers Thune to McDonald's because of his state of mind, age, and buying power. He doesn't like the McDonald's logo, which he thinks can only be described as "hideous," a word he normally prefers not to use, for stylistic reasons. The Majorstua post office on the other hand can be characterized as both sedate and venerable, yes, even to the degree that the new decor in the entry hall doesn't deprive the ladies in Majorstua of their legendary delicacy and incredible ability to put up with all conditions of the roadway on Kirkeveien and the overcrowded premises of the bakeries in Majorstua when they exit the post office after cashing their welfare or pension checks. Over on the other side of the street, as you head up the right side of Kirkeveien to the stoplight at Suhms Gate: KA International, the Bjørke Agency, the Maternity Cabinet, the Miner, Paints for Everyone, Oriento, Kids Interior. Or a furniture store, which here at the edge of Oslo's most anonymous urban neighborhood advertises its international character, with subsidiaries and branches in Madrid, Oslo, London, Paris, and Stockholm; and when Armand sees this he might well add a few business connections for himself: Mexico City, Amman, Cairo, Budapest, Buenos Aires, now that he's enjoying being here in this mood when the relationship between time and reality is somewhat delayed. Next to him is the Bjørke Agency, a specialty store featuring fireproof and burglar-proof safes, including gun cabinets. It's next to a shop for pregnant women that sells so-called maternity dresses, and which with a coquettish glance at its neighbor that sells burglarproof safes and gun cabinets, calls itself the Maternity Cabinet. Next door on the other side is the Miner, which sells jewelry and crystals taken from the mountains by the miner himself. After that comes Paints for Everyone, and then a small Asian café, Oriento, before the Bjørke Agency reinvigorates the passersby, including Armand V. strolling up the street, before he passes Trudvangveien, where Kids Interior occupies the corner. Still not a soul anywhere. Armand crosses to the other side, to a building with no shops on the ground floor. Cars are whooshing up and down. What could be hiding behind that worn-out facade? Does anyone live there? Armand can confirm, after having walked this long detour to and from his son's place a number of times over the past six months, that he has never seen a single person standing outside the entrance to any of these rental apartments, fiddling with their keys; nor has he ever seen the street door close with a cheerful bang as someone emerges from the inner courtyard, male or female, young or old, child or grown-up. But Pizza Pancetta in the courtyard next door is open. There are staff inside too. People making pizzas and the waitstaff. And in Studio Renée, a barber and beauty shop. Haircutters there, of course. Inside Driver Training Specialist, a man sits at a desk in the middle of the shop reading a newspaper. A steep basement stairway leads down to Rock Bottom Prices, and Armand crosses another street, this time Hammerstads Gate; he could have turned right here and would have been directly in front of the building where his son lives, but he doesn't. He crosses Hammerstads Gate, and walks along the sidewalk past the lovely facades of Kirkeveien Flowers and Bjørn Mathisen Antiques. In the florist's shop Armand notices several customers before he again crosses and continues up a block consisting of nothing but apartment buildings, before he recrosses the street again and enters a neighborhood with a nameless kiosk in a basement, then China Gifts, Thai Massage and Reflexology, and finally another apartment building with no shops on the ground floor; there the traffic lights at the intersection of Suhms Gate are blinking, oddly close, changing regularly, automatically, between green and red. Before he turns right onto Suhms Gate, he sends a long glance down Kirkeveien, across vacant lots and knolls to where the white building of the Norwegian Broadcasting System glows, and Armand looks at his watch to check whether it's showing the same time as the clock at the top of the building. Down there it's another world, which lies closer to Armand's world than the areas he has just strolled through; down there the same gentle promise it used to have still holds.

The last time Armand went to pay his son's rent to the old widow on the first of the month, he took the tram to Majorstua as usual, crossed the street by the central tram stop, and started up the right side of Kirkeveien, past the branch of the elegant Thune goldsmith shop, then McDonald's, and the Majorstua post office until he crossed Ole Vigs Gate. Spring had arrived, and Armand was dressed in a new light-colored, almost white, spring coat. He was wearing elegant, pointy-toed Italian walking shoes, made from very thin leather. Around his neck he wore a scarf of pure cashmere wool because of the chilly air, which he especially felt whenever he moved out of the warm springtime sunshine and into the shadows. Armand was a stylish man in his sixties, which was evident as he passed this row of buildings housing Thune the goldsmith, McDonald's, and the Majorstua post office, where there were often the beginnings of a crowd, before crossing Ole Vigs Gate and entering the more sparsely populated area up toward the stoplight at Suhms Gate. He walked past the row of various businesses between Ole Vigs Gate and Trudvangveien, crossed Trudvangveien, and continued toward the intersection of Hammerstads Gate. Cars were whizzing past on both sides of the center divider, and Armand's heart was pumping steadily in the chilly spring sunshine as he walked in his Italian shoes along the dry asphalt. The constant hum of the big city. The desolate aura of this neighborhood, Armand's heart pounding. That's how it should have been yesterday, when he passed by Pizza Pancetta and Studio Renée haircutters for ladies and gents. He noticed that there was a customer in the hair salon, a woman in her fifties sitting under the hood of a hair dryer and reading a magazine. Armand couldn't help stopping to peer discreetly into the salon. He took a couple of steps back so as not to stand directly in front staring into the salon, pausing a few steps to the right of the shop window. What did this remind him of? It reminded him of something, that's why he'd stopped. An incident from another time, in another city, not in Norway, but in some different country? He couldn't quite recall, but could it have been in Madrid? In spite of everything? But he stopped trying to remember, because now he witnessed an unusual sight. A young man came running down Kirkeveien at full speed. Running as if his life depended on it. Two men were chasing him, but they were heavier and stockier than the guy running ahead, so they couldn't catch him but fell farther and farther behind, even though they too were running at what was full speed for them. Behind those two men, farther up the street, halfway to the intersection at Suhms Gate, Armand spied an elderly woman. She had straightened up and stood howling at the sky. The first man was now approaching Armand. He was so pale, but he was fast on his feet. As he was about to pass by, Armand couldn't resist. He wanted to do something, so he stuck out his left foot with his elegant Italian shoe right in front of the running youth, who tripped and fell headlong to the sidewalk. Armand discreetly withdrew his foot and continued up Kirkeveien, toward the stoplight at Suhms Gate, as if nothing had happened. His foot hurt, of course, but he ignored the pain and made sure to keep walking with no sign of a limp. The two middle-aged, rather corpulent men puffed past him as Armand kept walking. Up the street he could still see the old lady howling at the sky, and he set off toward her.

But then he changed his mind. Instead of crossing Hammerstads Gate and continuing up toward Åsaveien, he stopped and turned around. He saw that the pale youth had been pulled to his feet by the two middle-aged, rather pudgy men, and one of them was holding the kid's hands behind his back while the other was talking on his cell phone. On the sidewalk lay an old-fashioned handbag, the contents partially strewn into the street. Armand heard sirens and saw the police cars coming down Kirkeveien, and saw them pull to a stop at the curb. Armand turned around again and on the way up Kirkeveien to the stoplight at Suhms Gate he passed the old lady, who still stood rooted to the spot, but she had stopping howling and her gaze was fixed on something far down Kirkeveien. He passed her quietly, without offering even a word of consolation, which he probably should have done. At the stoplight he turned right, and at Schultz' Gate he turned right again onto the block where his son rented a room. His good mood had vanished, and he was brooding intensely over what had just happened, and his own role in it.

2 B. Yes, he knew Oslo like the inside of his own pants pocket, so to speak. That was an expression a lot of people used back then, in the sixties, and he didn't know why, because what in the world did it mean to know your own pocket? Could it be that it was intimately associated with the concept of "pocket pool," which was also used a lot in those days, so that one expression had no meaning without being associated with the other? Because young men never had much in their front pockets. Usually no more than the keys to their own rented room and a handkerchief. They kept their wallet in a back pocket, which isn't the same as the front one, since there are two pockets in front and that is where they would stick their hands, and then they might have occasion to play pocket pool, as it was then called, as a sort of distraction. So, he knew Oslo like the proximity of his own dick in a game of distraction.

---

3. The living. And the dead. It's difficult to express. Maybe it's like this: even though there have never been as many people living on earth as there are now, still, more of them are dead than alive. As the years go by we approach this majority and the last journey that all of us will take.

4. Something else happened that day too. After Armand had paid the old widow a month's rent for his son's room, he left the building and headed down toward Bogstadveien. He walked along Ole Vigs Gate to Industrigata and kept going. He glanced at his watch and saw that he didn't have a lot of time, because he had an important meeting in less than an hour. But he still thought he had time to walk. If he went down Bogstadveien and Hegdehaugsveien, and then cut through the Palace Park past the Royal Palace, he could make it to his appointment without exerting himself. He liked to walk. It's what he liked best, just as he had liked tearing around Oslo back when he was a student forty years ago, and this cold and sunny spring day had reminded him of that. But these days he walked for the exercise, not for the sake of the hunt and the chance of possible (or impossible) happiness. Oddly enough, he thought he was more observant now than he'd been back then. When he reached Bogstadveien, he spotted Hagemann on the other side of the street, so he decided to go over and say hello.

Hagemann was standing by the modern-looking office building at the corner of Bogstadveien and Industrigata, which was also the site of a sort of shopping arcade with fashionable boutiques and the like. Hagemann was standing on the sidewalk next to a table and handing out flyers to passersby. Armand didn't know Hagemann very well, but he'd been hearing about him for years, ever since they were both at the university. They hadn't studied in similar fields, but they'd met through mutual friends. Armand's most vivid memory of Hagemann was associated with the man's girlfriend, an extraordinary and beautiful red-haired woman. Later on they got married. That's what Armand had heard. After graduation Armand hadn't run into Hagemann again until the mideighties, when Hagemann held an important position in one of the prominent parties of which Norway has so many. Unfortunately he eventually got mixed up in a shady scandal, which involved financial irregularities, though its significance may have been blown all out of proportion. At any rate, Hagemann was convicted of embezzlement and spent two or three years in prison before he was released. Some of his former political cronies helped him find a job at some office or warehouse, and now and then Armand would run into him, though infrequently, and he would always stop for a chat. Hagemann's remarkably beautiful redhead had stuck by him through the revelation, scandal, trial, and prison sentence. When he was released he moved back home with her and their two children, and possibly, Armand wasn't sure, they had moved to a less expensive apartment because their financial situation had naturally suffered, most likely to an extreme degree. But after a few years they ended up divorced. By that time the children were grown and had moved out. Since then, Hagemann had lived alone, presumably in the same neighborhood, because it was here, in the vicinity of Bogstadveien, that Armand had now run into him once again.

They always took the time for a chat. Exchanged views, actually. Armand never tried to pump Hagemann about his private life, so he knew no more than what he'd heard from others, and this put him at a disadvantage. Now he crossed the street, choosing to jaywalk instead of obeying the city's admonition to cross at the light, which would have forced him to stand and wait for the light to change in order to cross Industrigata, then wait for the other light to change to cross Bogstadveien, and then wait for the green light to cross Industrigata on the lower side of Bogstadveien. No, he stepped right out into the street, after first making sure that no tram was about to run him down and that the cars were so far away in both directions that they wouldn't hit him either, or just miss him and honk angrily; he reached the opposite side of the street, where Hagemann, who had seen him coming, approached, and they shook hands.

Armand knew what sort of flyers Hagemann was distributing and what sort of materials he had on the table beside him. They were flyers that strongly opposed the Death Penalty in the United States. Today they dealt with an individual whose execution was scheduled within a week, and Hagemann was collecting signatures in favor of a reprieve. Piled on a simple, worn-out card table were brochures, photo magazines, books, and other items. There were statistics on how many people in the U.S. were on death row and waiting to be executed. How many had been executed since 1976, when the Death Penalty had been reintroduced. Photographs of prisoners on death row. Photographs of those who had been executed. Armand had understood that Hagemann was no longer employed. He had taken early retirement, and Hagemann's old friend the attorney Julius Hansen had helped him to obtain a good pension, after navigating a lot of red tape.

"I used to make pretty good money," Hagemann said now, and mentioned Julius Hansen, the attorney. "You probably remember him. Well, they finally gave in." That was when he'd started distributing information protesting the Death Penalty.

But his involvement had started well before that. In fact, it must have started not long after Hagemann had been released from prison, or maybe a few years later.

Armand shared a number of opinions with Hagemann. Including his view of the Death Penalty in the States, but Armand had to tread lightly there, considering his profession. The Death Penalty in America wasn't really something he wanted to discuss on the street. But he couldn't help voicing his indignation over some of the cases that Hagemann showed him. The photo series from all the states that had used the electric chair made a huge impression on him. As well as the lethal injection chambers. And the glass walls where witnesses could watch the victim. As well as the last meals. The developmentally challenged who had been executed, along with the insane, and there were minors who were put to death. But Armand tried to change the subject to other topics they could discuss. Today, for instance, Armand thought he ought to tell Hagemann about what had happened just earlier, when for reasons he didn't entirely understand he had tripped a junkie purse-snatcher so that the youth landed on his face and the two men who were chasing him caught him and called the police. He wanted to hear Hagemann's opinion, what he thought was his motive—Armand's motive, that is, not the pale junkie's motive. But as he started to tell him about this incident he stopped, because his account would include mention of the arrest, the police, and inevitably the trial and verdict. So he said instead that he had just been paying rent for his son, who was in the military.

"He's a soldier now," Armand said. "All of a sudden he enlisted, and I thought he should keep his rented room to use when he's on leave; a grown son shouldn't have to live with his father when he's home, or with his mother for that matter," Armand said, recalling that once he had asked Hagemann: "Do you see your kids nowadays?" And remembering that he could have bitten his tongue because the question was so tactless, that's not what he should have asked. Instead: "How are your kids?" That was something altogether different, with no insinuations like the first question, which revealed a superior attitude toward Hagemann, implying that he didn't see his kids very often, something that was really none of his business unless Hagemann brought up the topic.

It's obvious that Armand really wanted to treat Hagemann with respect. Hagemann who had fallen. What Armand had realized, and he thought this was the remarkable thing about Hagemann, was that it was his time in prison, those two or three years, that had led him to protest against the Death Penalty in the U.S. with greater intensity each passing year, it seemed. It was in his capacity as a humbled ex-convict that he reacted to the Death Penalty in the U.S.A. He would prefer life in prison, then he'd at least be alive, thought the former convict Hagemann, who, it must be assumed, had scarcely had a chance to forget that he was an ex-convict, at least not for many minutes at a time. Everyone viewed him that way and felt sorry for him, even Armand. He knew that everyone felt the same, and there was nothing he could do about it. Once Hagemann had been a trusted politician, a member of one of Norway's foremost parties, but he had betrayed this trust in order to feather his own nest. There was no question, he had to take the fall. But was it any wonder that it was as a member of the party supporting a world power (which allowed the Death Penalty) that Hagemann had become a leading figure; support that provided the final, decisive proof that he and his party existed, or lived in the world of reality, and that after his release he used so much of his remaining strength to oppose that policy? Armand didn't know. He tried, as he was doing now, to challenge Hagemann a little about the political position of the United States in the world today, under its new administration, but received merely a polite, almost indifferent response to the view Armand was trying to elicit. Hagemann didn't seem interested, or at least he preferred not to appear particularly interested.

They did exchange opinions, although mostly about neutral topics like the weather and geography, historical phenomena from the point in time when those of us most obsessed with modernity began identifying anything before January 1, 2000, as the last century, especially relating to international issues, which included the death sentence in the United States. They stood there on the corner of Bogstadveien and Industrigata, in front of a modern office building from the aforementioned previous century. They also discussed the Champions League, and soccer in general on TV. Armand was enjoying chatting with Hagemann, who would occasionally accost a passerby and hand him a flyer about the latest execution in the States. But when Armand glanced at his watch he realized that he was running out of time. The important conference at the Department was going to start in fifteen minutes. Fortunately there was a cab stand right around the corner, so he could make it in time. The two gentlemen in their sixties said goodbye and shook hands, and as they did, Armand was reminded of his own

Appointment back when he was forty-two. It was around the time when Hagemann had met his downfall, almost at the same time. He wondered whether Hagemann might have been arrested on the very day when he received his Appointment. More than twenty years ago they had both been successful men in the public life of their small country, one employed in the civil service, the other leading a political life. Then one of them suffered a merciless fall, and the other received an Appointment. Is it therefore possible to regard these two gentlemen taking their leave of each other, on a residential street corner in a little northern European capital, as representing no less than two different fates? Whether Armand was capable of viewing himself as representing a fate, however, is doubtful. But was that how he viewed Hagemann? Or did Armand view Hagemann, despite his attraction to him, as mere coincidence? For me, writing this, it's important to ask such questions.

———

5. Is a novel something that has already been written, and is the author merely the one who finds it, laboriously digging it out? I have to admit that with each passing year I have come to realize more and more clearly that I am enveloped in such a notion. But who wrote the novel originally, if I'm simply the one who discovered and excavated it? This is a comment to a place in the text above that deals with, or conceals, a metaphysical concern of the highest order.

5 B. It is timely to ask this question because a finished novel, authored and published under my name, was actually completed

by me as well. How many drafts do I write before a particular section turns out the way it should in the published book? At least twenty! Over and over again. I keep on until it looks the way I want it to look. I keep revising until it's the way it should be. As if it were predicted beforehand. Sometimes I'm surprised, but weren't those surprises also forecast in advance?

Most of these drafts aren't very interesting, they're part of a normal procedure in which something that isn't very good eventually finds its proper form through laborious effort. Once it evolves into something good, it becomes crystal clear that it's much better than it was in the initial attempt. But there are also instances when it's not so clear at first glance, and even though these instances might be negligible in number, they're the ones on which we now have to train our spotlight.

It's a matter of those instances where there is apparently no particular qualitative difference between the first attempt and the final one, the one that remains standing; yes, in some cases I may even suspect that from an outside viewpoint the first version was actually just as good. It's a matter of one section that has nothing wrong with it and another section that has nothing wrong with it either, except for the fact that in the first case I say: No, I don't think so, and in the second I say: Yes! Finally!

What standard do I use to make such strongly contradictory judgments of clear disapproval vs. firm acclamation? Because that's what I'm doing, it's a fact. I *could* have written that I don't know, yet I have a sense the novel I'm working on is already done, and my task is to lead it forward. Let's cut to the chase: I'm well aware of why I rejected the first draft. It's because no matter how well written it may be, no matter how high the literary temperature, etc., etc., I could just as well have written the exact opposite. All that's missing is necessity. That and nothing more.

There's also another circumstance on which I have to shine the spotlight. Sometimes I wake up in the night, having denounced my own novel, as far as I've gotten with it. This will happen in the dream from which I have just emerged, and I realize that I have to deal with the consequences. In a waking state I noticed nothing, but at night, having sunk into a dream state, it churns and churns inside of me. I have to get up, although it's the middle of the night, and retrieve my manuscript. I slowly read back until I find the spot where the whole thing went off the rails. It might be thirty or forty pages back, and let's say a month of hard work has passed since I've noticed any detours. I'll have to start over from that point. It would have seemed incomprehensible to others that I'm now throwing away these pages, and to me as well, until I rejected these pages in my dreams, and now I understand why I'm doing it. Maybe it could be called intuition. But what is intuition really? That I intuitively had the whole novel ready even before I began to write down the first line, and that it clearly signals from deep inside my bad dreams, time after time, when I've gone astray?

5 c. The novel takes place partly in Oslo, partly in the high mountains, and partly during an ocean voyage. And large parts of it take place abroad. The novel is invisible to the author in the sense that he is unable to write it. He can see it, see into it, but he can't write it. He has to relate to, and also write, "the text up there," or "the text out there." It obviously deals with Armand V., whom the author pretends to know, or pretends to

have known. The shape the novel takes is unknown, since the author at some early point refused to enter into it and lead it forward.

5 D. This novel, which is invisible, we can call the original novel. In contrast to what is here on paper, which is the novel as it now exists. It consists of footnotes to the original novel. The compositional principle of the present text cannot be deduced from the form of the original novel, but it must be sought, and has already been sought by the author, through that which exists, i.e., the footnotes, which, unlike the original novel, have been written by the author, meaning me.

5 E. It is indisputable that this novel, the sum of the footnotes to the original novel, which is invisible because the author refused to delve into it and make it his own, is about Armand V. It is most probable that the original novel also dealt with Armand V., at least that's what the author asserts, based on the tiny glimpses he claims to have had of it, that which he believes to have perceived, in part crystal clear, in part as a faint flicker. The fact that I will later claim that it's far from certain that Armand V. has the same name in the original novel, "the text out there," as here below in the footnotes, is an entirely different matter. What *is* germane, however, is that it is by no means certain that the theme of this novel is the same as that of the original novel. I am not even thinking solely of the extent to which the themes are identical, but rather to what extent they have anything to do with each other at all. Yet the footnotes remain footnotes to this unwritten, possibly incommensurable novel.

5 F. Why this disavowal? Why does the author refuse to enter into the original novel, and lead it forward, word by word, the way he usually does? Put more directly: Why don't I do it, since I'm the one who's writing this? Why do I refuse, and why have I been refusing for almost two years now? Because I am no longer capable of writing down the novel I have been given the privilege to dig up, but must be content with writing footnotes to this work, in which I obviously no longer believe. It must have something to do with my age. Long ago I passed the age of sixty, and I'm occupied with looking forward, not to the future, but to the end. I can no longer change the world, but I can terminate it.

5 G. I no longer think that I'm in any condition to write novels the way I used to. My day is over. It appears that I talk about "the original novel," or "the text up above," or "the text out there." But what about the novel's Plan? It no longer exists. I can no longer refer to the Plan, and why not? Because I have no future in what I write. Even my darkest novels were not without a future. They may have been without hope, but they weren't without a future. Now they have no future; that time is past, and now my time is up. So what do I do? ... This.

5 H. I'm so free that I suspect someone might be playing a prank on me, as if I begin to dig up what is now available to me as the original novel, or the Plan. It's possible I'm being completely fooled by someone or other, or rather by something or other. In order to avoid that, I'm proceeding with this. Responding in like manner, as they say.

51. An ocean voyage. The eternal cabin girl, the so-called waitress. Conversations on board. The ship's route. A November cruise off the coast of northern Europe. He received an invitation.

It's an alternative ocean voyage. The one that occurs simultaneously, in the text above, follows a different course than the one taking place here; for example, the ports of call and the characters that appear here, except for the protagonist himself, are different from those that appear up in the novel, in that story itself.

_____

6. The Appointment took place before the King at the cabinet meeting. He was quite young to be appointed as an ambassador, only forty-two. But one of the reasons was that he knew the region well from before, since he had served there previously, as the ambassador's secretary, and he'd served as a ministerial councilor in two of the neighboring countries.

Just before he departed, his credentials were transferred to the foreign ministry, where he received them in order to hand them over in person to the head of state in the country to which he was now appointed ambassador. It was a small country located in the desert in the Middle East. The country was separated from one neighbor by a river that bore the same name as the state to which he had been appointed ambassador. He arrived at the capital of this country and was picked up at the airport and taken to the Norwegian Embassy. Here he spent a few days while he waited to be summoned to the Palace to deliver his credentials. When the call came, he got into the back seat of the official Norwegian Embassy limousine and was driven to the Palace, while the attaché case containing the credentials rested solemnly on his lap. At the Palace he was led into a hall to wait, where a number of other ambassadors were also waiting. One by one they were formally summoned and ushered into an adjoining room. At last it was Armand's turn. He was escorted into the audience hall of the Palace, where he personally delivered the letter from the King of Norway to this country's head of state. The King of Jordan accepted it, offering Armand a few friendly words. He was now Norway's ambassador to Jordan.

---

7. In the mid-1960s, Paul Buer and his best friend Armand arrived in Oslo to study at the university at Blindern. Paul ended up among the physical scientists, known as the "realists," while Armand settled down with the "humanists." After two years they could be found at their respective tables with their respective cohorts in the enormous Frederikke student cafeteria, far apart from each other. Armand hung out at the eastern end of the cafeteria, which was closer to the humanities buildings named for Henrik Wergeland and Sophus Bugge, while Paul sat at the far west end by the wall, at a big round table, and ate his brown-bag lunch among his colleagues. Occasionally the two would run into each other in the cafeteria line. The lines could be long, and Armand would go from one line to another to find the shortest, which was often in the part of the cafeteria where Paul hung out. When they met like this and had to wait with their trays in their hands, Armand would often invite Paul to come sit at his table. In the course of their years of study, Paul

would sometimes, on his own initiative, venture over to the other end to join Armand, but Armand hardly ever left his table to sit with the physical scientists.

Paul felt shy whenever he sat with Armand and his fellow students. He couldn't manage to say a single word. He had developed an inferiority complex because he knew he'd look like a fool if he said anything. During those years when he sporadically sat at Armand's table he uttered very few words, and if he searched his memory he could probably remember them all. The only times he spoke were when one of the other humanists tried to be kind to him because he was Armand's friend and asked him a direct question, and then he might reply: "Yes, we've been friends since we were kids," "mathematics (and later geophysics)," "yes, that wouldn't surprise me," "no, I wouldn't think so!" and "yes, I agree completely." Otherwise he mostly paid attention to Armand, with whom he tried to keep a conversation going, and Armand tried to do the same but couldn't really manage it because suddenly he would have to keep interrupting their private exchanges by calling out across the table some comment to something the others were discussing, and this would make Paul feel even more superfluous. There was always a bunch of women at Armand's table, something that couldn't be said about Paul Buer's own table with the physical scientists, and that made Paul feel shy, coupled with the fact that everyone was so impressive, including the female humanities students. They knew how to express themselves with such wit. Which really wasn't so strange, Paul told himself, since that's what they're studying, learning how to express themselves, even in foreign languages. It's different with us, who usually end up in what are to everyone else incomprehensible combinations of symbols, sort of like the way Donald Duck would swear in the comics when I was a kid. That's what he would think (afterwards, always afterwards, when he got back to his own table, or to his own seminar in the Physics building on the other side of Blindernveien).

The humanities students were self-confident. Every time Paul ventured over to join Armand, carrying his lunch on a tray, one of them would be sitting there reading *Dagbladet* and quoting something from the editorial, either offering enthusiastic comments or sarcastic criticism. These were the men of today! They were critical of contemporary Norwegian literature, which they did not read, except for books by Johan Borgen and Tarjei Vesaas, but those guys were getting up there in years. They predicted that soon a new batch of writers would emerge that would engage their interest, writers who would take the new literature in Sweden and Denmark as their role models. Just wait, they said, the time is ripe. Norway can't continue to lag behind much longer. Or else they discussed philosophy and society, with a flood of references, and everyone put in their two cents, asserting their importance over everyone else's opinions, except for a few who remained silent, including Paul Buer, but he couldn't be counted, other than as a good childhood friend of Armand's. They have the gift of gab, Paul thought, but damn it, how great to be able to talk like that.

Armand had a way with words, he always had, but now he'd come into his own, you might say, and the others received him with open arms. Armand thrived like never before among the humanities students, and not least among the women studying

French and art history. He'd confessed in private to Paul that he found them most attractive.

"Why?" Paul asked.

"Because they think mostly about their own beauty, and less about their studies." This was precisely an answer that somehow seemed more enticing, even exciting, to Paul Buer, and for a moment he was angry at himself for not choosing to study humanities instead of physical sciences. Not merely because Armand had developed an affable personality. That's why he always let Armand choose the film they were going to see when they went to the movies together, which they did quite often. They would go to the Gimle and see the newest French and Italian and Polish movies.

"That's the fourth time I've seen this one," Armand said when they came out of the Gimle after seeing *Last Year at Marienbad*, "and it just gets better every time."

"I sure hope so," said Paul, "because honestly I thought it was really boring, except for the part when they acted out a scene from Ibsen's *Rosmersholm*."

"*Rosmer*, not *Rosmersholm*," said Armand. "Didn't you see the poster? It said *Rosmer*, not *Rosmersholm*, although Ibsen never wrote a play called *Rosmer*." So based on that detail, he began to interpret the film scene by scene for Paul. Then Paul said he liked *Blow-Up* better, especially the tennis match where they played with imaginary balls, but well, anyone could think up this stuff, he told Armand afterward.

"It's dumb to admit that you go to the Gimle to get horny," Armand replied. "It'll just backfire on you."

"But I did like *Blow-Up*," said Paul stubbornly, "a lot better than *8½*, which was *so slow*."

"But *8½* was so intensely white," Armand exclaimed, appalled at Paul's lack of development.

He kept recommending books for him to read. "You should read Kafka," he told him once.

"I've read him. He's good," Paul replied.

"Which one?"

"*The Trial*. I really liked it."

"So you understood it? Well, you must be really smart, because there aren't many people who admit they do," Armand responded, referring to the other humanities students. "What did you think of it? I suppose you know that people argue about whether *The Trial* is a deeply metaphysical work, or whether it was written by a joker."

"I think it's a metaphysical work," said Paul.

"Oh, you're only saying that because you don't know what a joke actually is. It's not what you think, it's way more complicated than that," Armand said with disdain.

When Armand scoffed like that, Paul never hesitated to rebut him if they were alone. At least on those occasions when Armand had been going at it for a while. And he wasn't afraid to take on Armand when he thought his literary friends had been acting too much like Holberg's Erasmus Montanus, as he expressed it. But then Armand might reply: "Erasmus Montanus was right. The world really is as flat as a pancake." That response would stop Paul short, but he would good-naturedly agree with Armand—good-naturedly because if he'd contradicted him, which he could have done, based on the fact that you have to say the world is not flat as a pancake, we cannot say that it is, then *he* would have ended up in an Erasmus Montanus position, so he agreed with Armand, which was as it should be. Odd, he thought, how easy it is to be fooled by this fine world. I'd always heard that Erasmus Montanus was a ridiculous figure, but Armand was right. It was the others who were wrong, which makes them ridiculous. No, it's important not to make overly hasty conclusions, especially when hanging out with people like Armand's friends. That's why Paul said that he thought they were genuinely spiritual, those who gathered at Armand's table, and that he was actually impressed, so impressed that he didn't dare say anything himself, even when he thought (rarely) that he had something to say. But then Armand contradicted him.

"Phooey," he said, "stop trying to pretend you're dumber than you are. You have to admit that all this is nothing but illusion. It's just something you've learned by heart, all of it. No need to be impressed. It's a cheap trick, that's all. Illusion!" he shouted. When Armand called it out as illusion Paul couldn't decide whether he meant it, or if it was nothing but a show put on for his friend, no matter how serious and intense he looked when he said it.

Apart from Armand, Paul didn't know anyone at the university in the early days. In engineering there was a guy from his hometown that he chatted with now and then, but otherwise he just hung out on his own, without feeling lonely. It wasn't until he'd been there a year that he found his spot at a table by the wall in the Frederikke student cafeteria. That's when he got to know Tor Erik Paulsen, who was in the same group with him, taking a math course. Tor Erik mentioned that his last name was Paulsen, and Paul was Paul, which he said with a grin, as if there should be some automatic connection, and Paul Buer got a little embarrassed. Some time later he was passing through the chess room in the basement of Frederikke, glancing at the games that were in progress, when he spied Tor Erik laying out chess pieces on a board. Tor Erik noticed Paul and waved him over. Now Paul and Paulsen were going to play a match, he said, as if he'd been sitting there waiting for him, and Paul again felt a bit embarrassed. In fact, Tor Erik hadn't been waiting for him specifically; he liked to come in here, find a table, set up the chessmen, and call over someone who came in, usually someone he knew. Because of the embarrassment that Paul felt, he ended up getting to know Paulsen, who in turn invited him to join his group of "realists," and Paul spent much of his free time with them in subsequent years.

In a way there was nothing special about this particular group. It was like a lot of other groups of friends among the science and engineering students at Blindern in those years. They would sit at the west end of Frederikke eating their bag lunches at noon, and then come back a few hours later, between three and four, to line up for dinner and wait their turn to eat meatballs with stewed red cabbage, or boiled cod with carrots.

They were serious and industrious students, goal-oriented, and most of them got good grades. They were largely introverted and taciturn, but in every group there was always one, or often two, who played the role of life of the party, telling jokes that they all laughed at, appreciating the humor. During the seven years Paul spent at the university among them, he hardly ever heard a serious conversation about life. It was a lively group that cultivated the lighthearted, witty, and trivial, in both cultural and social matters. At the same time there was something sad about these students that was hard to ignore. There was something stagnant about them, as if they were caught in a swamp that was sucking them down, and they couldn't get out. They were good at their studies, and several were quite gifted, but even they couldn't escape. Something was clinging to them. When it came right down to it, the most distinctive thing about them was that they were so ordinary. Why were they here, anyway? That's a question that had to be asked if you wanted to understand anything about Paul Buer and his like-minded cohorts, including the talented Jan Brosten.

So, why were they here? Or: Why weren't they someplace else? Like in Trondheim, at the NTH, the Norwegian Technical College, for example. That's where the civil engineers were usually trained. The ones who built bridges, skyscrapers, jumbo jets, automobiles, roads, and machines, and who sat on the boards of the companies that made all these things based on mathematics and physics. In other words, the subjects that the "realists" at Blindern were studying. Why weren't they all there, at the NTH? Several of them in Paul's circle had passed the *examen artium* (entrance exam) with scores high enough to be admitted to the NTH, but they hadn't bothered to apply. They wanted to stay here. As for those who hadn't had good enough grades to be admitted, why didn't they do like so many of their contemporaries and study abroad to be civil engineers? Because they didn't want to be civil engineers. They didn't want to study math and physics with the goal of taking their place as key performers in the midst of pulsating life. That's not what they wanted. Though they never wasted time speculating over this decision, we may establish that much. Their studies offered so many opportunities that could be developed in life, but they had rejected them all because they lacked the desire to participate in dynamic feats that society admired so highly. Instead they wanted to stay here, at Blindern. Studying the sciences. Which would probably turn them into math and physics teachers for lanky kids of seventeen before they were even thirty, and people would still regard them as teachers when they were well past fifty, or even sixty-five.

So that is the key question. Why did they want to stay here instead of there? It was their own peculiar nature, from which they would never be able to escape. For some reason they discovered they weren't suited to be civil engineers. For some reason they found they were more suited to be math teachers. It's obvious that Paul Buer and his cohorts had scant affinity for power. They possessed little of that kind of ambition. Power, and the gleam of it, did not tempt them at all, at least not enough to get them moving. And as a result you could say that they had no goals for their lives.

This did not mean that indifference was lodged deep in their souls. It didn't mean that everything was fluid in their lives, and they were merely floating with the stream. On the contrary. They were all so ordinary. Few had qualities that they openly presented to the world. Rather they seemed to be trying to conceal their traits. They preferred to remain as anonymous as possible. Paul Buer got along well with them. They were boring young men, viewed from the outside. They didn't live exciting lives, but that's what they enjoyed. They didn't look forward to anything particularly great, and they enjoyed that too. They liked sports and games, and if they won some insignificant victory in an insignificant game, or in an unimportant sports match, they would exult over their victory. Above all they wanted to live a good life, but without having to deal with excessive expectations. Unlike most other students they even thought the food at Frederikke was good, though they complained to each other that there was probably saltpeter in it, if only the others knew (the language majors, the social scientists, and the theologians, etc.).

Paul was glad that he'd found a group of like-minded students to hang out with after only a year of studying at Blindern. The group consisted of ten to twelve young men who were loosely associated because they would take their trays and hurry over to this table after they'd stood in the cafeteria line, and they always knew someone sitting there. Tor Erik Paulsen was usually the life of the party in the group, its bright light. Otherwise either Andersen or Pedersen took the lead. Or Hans Brun, who could be said to be a sort of leader, or chairman, because whenever he was present he influenced the mood with his boring way of speaking. Yet he came from a renowned family of academics, and he was himself a top student, so his words carried a certain weight. Not least because Jan Brosten, with whom Paul would eventually become strongly linked, seldom took the lead, speaking only if directly addressed, and then his words made the biggest impression.

Hans Brun often used to interrupt Paulsen's witticisms with an incisive remark, usually taken from some proverb. By this he intended to show that he had a good grasp of language and was able to counter Paulsen's rather cheap jokes, which the rest of the group frequently tired of hearing ad infinitum. Hans's humor was of the type that led to pronouncements like: "high they hang and pissed they are," "don't sell the pelt before you shoot the bear," and "it's only temporary, said the fox as he was being skinned." He was very good at inserting these proverbs at the appropriate place, and always as a pointed commentary to something someone else had said, usually Paulsen. Sometimes Paul Buer was the target of these remarks, and then he'd feel so embarrassed that it would be a while before he'd dare offer his opinion, or say anything at all instead of just sitting there and waiting, as he felt was his duty, and most of the others felt the same.

Eventually Paul Buer understood that the group had largely been recruited by Hans Brun and Jan Brosten. It was Paulsen, the "life of the party," and not Hans Brun or Jan Brosten, who had brought in Paul, and that was largely an exception; yet oddly enough he was accepted, probably in the name of tolerance. At any rate this led to Andersen and Pedersen bringing in a couple of friends who became loosely associated with their table. But the main thing was that it was everyone's connection to Hans Brun or Jan Brosten that brought them all together. And this relationship was based on knowledge, or a longing for knowledge. They were keenly aware that they were here to study, and to take their exams. They all wanted the best grades possible. They were industrious students, all of them, working to understand the laws of the outside world, in which they had absolutely no desire to participate. They had gotten to know each other in study groups. Hans Brun, for example, had offered to help Andersen with a math problem that was baffling him, and Jan Brosten had patiently shown Pedersen how to understand a problem in theoretical physics, while a third person had displayed a solid mastery regarding the use of a mathematical formula for a certain problem in methodology, and Hans Brun or Jan Brosten had sought out this third man, who may have been Paulsen or Gunnar Ingebrigtsen, and in this way gratitude and kindness developed into a mutual yet shy openness, a sympathetic gesture that might turn into a friendship, expressed in the sentence, "Now I get it," or "Now I understand," connecting the listener, that is, the one who revealed his objective insight, to the one who received it. In conjunction with all this, it shouldn't be ignored that the symbology of mathematics points to the farthest reaches of space, conveying a meaningful interpretation of such, and that ever since the earliest times a preoccupation with mathematics has been associated with the search for, and even the worship of, "God." "God?"

That's not what you would think if you listened to the conversations around that table, not even when the talk turned to professional matters. You would get the impression that above all they were looking forward to finishing their studies and obtaining positions as schoolteachers of math and physics and doing a lot of joking around with their pupils. They pictured their future teaching jobs as an endless series of bright days during which they entertained their future pupils with fun experiments. They indulged in imagining how they would tell amusing stories, for example the one about an egg. If you hurl a raw egg with all your might into the air, it will fly very high before falling back down. And when it does fall, it won't shatter, incredibly enough (provided the surface is flat and not sharp). Knowing about this, and also knowing that they would be demonstrating it for coming generations, was one of the countless joys of that group, and everyone concurred, even Hans Brun, especially him, but also Jan Brosten, right from the start, much to Paul Buer's astonishment (Paul himself was the only one who didn't contribute to collecting these fun experiments).

As far as that goes, Paul occasionally had a feeling that the main focus of the science departments was in viewing mathematics and physics as a game. A diversion. It protected the students from real life; in fact they used it to hide not only from themselves but from the reality in which, in spite of everything, they found themselves. This fixation could be seen as related to the eagerness displayed by this same group for measuring time and height, calculating points, noting the lap times in skating races, and studying the change in soccer schedules from one week to the next. Paul shared the group's interest in schedules, scores, and records to the highest degree; in fact many people might call him a sports nut, and yet he thought this was a profane or unacceptable reduction, even a perversion, of the very nature of mathematics and physics, somewhat in the same vein as the intense feeling of joy which he personally might experience—though finding himself still at a low level on the endless rungs of mathematics that had to be climbed to achieve greater clarity with each rung—whenever he solved an equation or suddenly produced a formula all on his own, and the numbers would appear, shining and simple, exact and irresistible. Of course it was impossible to sit at that table in Frederikke every day and talk about such an intense joy, which they had all experienced, and yet they felt compelled to try and hide it, transforming it into boisterous enthusiasm, an intense but empty zeal, for sports, and an obstinate emphasis on amusing natural phenomena, all of which could sometimes provoke in Paul, once again, a deep embarrassment.

It was also a big leap from mathematics and the heaven-defying formulas of theoretical physics to the way these students related to the human phenomenon that had, after all, developed these mathematical symbols, which now made it possible to hurl man-made objects into outer space, according to a specified plan. Unfortunately, it's impossible to ignore the fact that they had great difficulty focusing for any lengthy period of time, and with a certain degree of concentration, on human topics such as art and literature, history and psychology. They spoke for the most part in generalities. They actually took pleasure in spouting readily accepted opinions, which represented for them a way of expressing themselves in a relevant and healthy manner. They claimed something was sensible if the whole point was for them to view it as sensible; they regarded something as amusing if they were supposed to view it as amusing; and they allowed themselves to become thoroughly indignant if they were meant to become indignant, and their anger was unflinchingly genuine. Similarly, they allowed themselves to be moved by all the phenomena they read about, if they were supposed to be moved by them. Yet fierce disagreement would occasionally arise at the table when human phenomena came under discussion. Then two readily acceptable opinions might clash, and such a conversation would frequently devolve into nothing more than squabbling, since one person would become so enamored of his own readily acceptable opinion that he would do his utmost to skewer someone else's readily acceptable opinion, for which he ultimately developed such scorn that he could label it immoral or logically reprehensible.

When the group openly discussed themselves or others at the table, this same perspective held true. They found a great, identifiable joy in the fact that each person behaved exactly as they had predicted he would. For example, whenever Andersen left the table without removing the tray with his dirty plate, cutlery, and coffee cup, the others would yell at him to come back and get it.

"Typical Andersen," they'd say afterward, almost elated that once again Andersen had behaved in such a typical Andersen manner, as only Andersen could do. And by "typical Andersen," they didn't mean merely that he had once again left the table without taking his tray to the clearing area; no, they meant that the way Andersen was behaving at this moment caused them to recognize him from similar situations that had occurred in other places and in completely different contexts, entitling them to call out "typical Andersen," even though this might actually have been the first time Andersen had forgotten his tray when he got up and left the table. And the merriment that was evident in their voices when they looked at each other and exclaimed "typical Andersen" also revealed the joy they derived from reaching such conclusions about Andersen, especially if it was the first time he had forgotten his tray of dirty dishes, because then they knew, and in a most convincing manner, that when Andersen forgot to remove his tray, it was not mere coincidence but rather an incident which, based on what Andersen had previously done in the seminar rooms, the laboratory, the gymnasium, and at the chessboard, represented typical behavior on his part, and for them it was a great joy to recognize this behavior and this person named Andersen in a new situation. This is Andersen, and we take great pleasure in recognizing him again. In other words, there was no small amount of warmth and generosity in their passion for these types of characterizations. Because the joy of recognition eclipses and mutes the criticism that necessarily arises when a man shirks his duty to carry his tray of dirty dishes to the clearing area. This was reinforced when recognition of the typical no longer concerned typical behavior but instead had to do with psychology. Because subsequently, after Andersen forgot to remove his tray and was called back to the table, he picked up the tray and gave a disarming shrug, and this too was "typical Andersen," because they had often noticed him do this whenever he was caught out, had suffered a loss, made a mistake, or was guilty of some misunderstanding. On those occasions he would play the innocent, smooth things over, or else, like now, he would give a disarming shrug in order to trivialize or diminish, or if possible even cover up, the whole matter. Recognizing this psychological trait in its various guises as "typical Andersen" always aroused greater joy than the criticism or aloofness, which discovery of the mistake, loss, neglect, or misunderstanding deserved, and thus you might say there was something unflinchingly tolerant about their view of their fellow human beings. Various qualities such as "greed," "quarrelsomeness," "avarice," "obstinacy," and "arrogance" were all censured and yet accepted with an underlying warmth when noted as "typical Andersen," "typical Hans Brun," "typical Per Arne Pedersen," "typical Ingebrigtsen," "typical Paulsen," "typical Jan Brosten," and for that matter even "typical Buer." By this they meant they possessed a system of concepts that was sufficient to reference the personal traits of those with whom they were in daily contact. The problem for them was to connect Andersen's existence with the actual person named Andersen, whom they could see but who was not identical with his existence. Andersen's existence was a mystery that was linked to the person Andersen and his way of being, and yet not identical with it. The person himself was clear enough. Look, here comes Andersen in his own tall manifestation, six feet two inches above sea level, 150 pounds, a real beanpole, carrying his tray as he heads over to their table. Look boys, here comes Andersen! He was easy to spot; they recognized him from a distance of over one hundred sixty feet, looming above a forest of other people. But how were they supposed to connect Andersen-ness to this person named Andersen coming toward them? Andersen was more than the person Andersen, with his stooping posture, his neighing laugh, and his fogged-up glasses; this Andersen-ness, which they immediately perceived as attached to the person Andersen, as something that followed Andersen the person like a vague shadow, like his personality, was what they tried to capture, calling it "typical Andersen."

But what was their own attitude on being called "typical Paulsen," "typical Ingebrigtsen," "typical Jan Brosten," even "typical Buer" for that matter? All indications are that they accepted the fact that others used the concept of "typical" when referring to them. Even Paul Buer accepted it, although it wasn't something he liked to think about. And by the way, it's doubtful that any of the others spent much time considering the obvious likelihood that since they so spontaneously had exclaimed "typical Andersen" whenever Andersen behaved in

accordance with his personality, it meant the others, including Andersen, would also exclaim "typical Jan Brosten" behind
their backs whenever they showed off their own personalities.
This is the sort of thing that most people choose to dismiss if it
should happen to impinge on their consciousness. But it wasn't
only behind their backs that "typical Paulsen," etc., was said. It
was also put to them directly, taking the form of confrontation,
but also now, as in the case of Andersen, with an underlying
friendliness in the voice. To have thrown in your face a phrase
like: "how typical of you, Buer," was something you just had to
endure. Plain and simple. Even though very few people liked
it. But for the most part you played along with the notion, for
a brief time involuntarily taking some sort of central role; you
good-naturedly put up with it, having been supposedly caught
revealing your true personality. Occasionally someone might
protest and deny what was deemed "typical" about him. This
might occur because he found the characterization extremely
unfair or exaggerated, and for a moment he would lose his com-
posure at once again being confronted with such a label. Yet
the person then risked hearing phrases such as: "typical of you,
Paulsen, to deny what everyone else sees," or "typical of you,
Paulsen, to complain," causing you to try to counter any weari-
some repetitions of highly unjust or exaggerated characterizations of yourself with great calm. At other times the superficial
nature of such characterizations could get on your nerves, and
you might be tempted to display fierce annoyance at this way of
repeatedly confronting you with a diminished view of yourself.
But usually you kept quiet and good-naturedly played along
with this superficial diminishing of the "I" that you experienced

from the inside. In spite of everything, this was an attempt by the others to pigeonhole you, a type of deep delving into your very existence, and hence this exaggerated one-sidedness and superficiality functioned as a means of protecting your own "I," your true "I," which had absolutely no wish to be exposed to the spotlight. Use of "typical," as applied to yourself, and not just to the others, protected the sense of reserve which, through all the noise and commotion, was a fundamental trait shared by this group of science students, a contributing factor which lent their personalities such a strong aura of anonymity.

Both the person who said "typical Andersen," "typical Pedersen," as well as the one who was singled out as "typical Andersen," "typical Pedersen," had a mutual interest in limiting the understanding of the human phenomenon in such things that could be expressed as "typical Andersen" and "typical Pedersen." They had no interest in those who shirked such classifications. Naked existence, as it may manifest in various grimaces, twitches, mutterings, and stammerings, was of no interest to them. Not even in the form of caricatures, which they then called harassment and was taboo at their table. Nor were they interested in naked existence as it manifests in reflection or self-reflection. They were solely preoccupied with the capacity of their friends to be recognized as "typical," which they viewed as what was particularly personal and unique about them.

For that reason, no one shouted "typical Paulsen" when a bomb was dropped at their table. He had been absent for a long time, and the others had begun to wonder what had happened. No one knew where he was, whether he'd fallen ill, had gone away, or any of the other possibilities that might have occurred to Paulsen. Until one day when Ingebrigtsen told them that he'd talked to someone from Paulsen's hometown, and this person said that Paulsen had returned home and was now working in an office there. The truth was that Paulsen, during the course of the three years he'd spent studying the sciences, had not taken a single exam, while acquiring a student debt as large as that acquired by those who had faithfully and regularly taken their exams. Finally, it had to stop. Paulsen's father had found out what was going on, and he immediately came to Oslo to bring his failed and indebted son back home, where he got him an office job so that he could start to pay off his student loans.

This horrified the others. Paulsen's empty chair screamed at them, and they shook their heads and lamented his fate. They could vividly imagine how it was to attend the university in Blindern day in and day out, pretending to be a student when in reality you were doing nothing at all.

"He must have been miserable," said Hans Brun, and everyone nodded as they recalled with horror the lively Paulsen who had spread such merriment around their table.

"But he has to take responsibility," added Jan Brosten, and to that they all nodded with knowing looks.

Why hadn't he said anything to them? Instead he had pretended that his studies were going fine, and none of them had actually checked to see if his name was on the exam lists which announced who had passed on those occasions when he claimed to have taken an exam.

"Passed, somewhere in the middle, and slightly toward the bottom," was what Paulsen had said whenever they asked him how a specific exam had gone.

"He must have suffered from exam anxiety," Jan Brosten decided, in his defense. But if so, why hadn't he consulted a psychologist, who could have cured his nerves? "If he'd asked me, that's the advice I would have given him," said Brosten. "Instead of going around wasting time for years," he added indignantly.

They had a hard time knowing how to take the news about Paulsen. There was something so awkward about it. He had presented himself as something other than he was, and that was how he'd gained access to their table, as one of them. He had made himself out to be an ordinary student of the sciences, when in reality he was a good-for-nothing because he was plagued by anxiety. And he'd sat at their table. And entertained them with his witty remarks. There was something intolerable about that, when they thought back on it. Yet at the same time they couldn't stop thinking about it. The whole episode was too upsetting, too distressing to be simply forgotten. Especially to be dismissed for good. At least that was the opinion of Gunnar Ingebrigtsen and Andersen, for example. So they made sure that Paulsen was remembered. First they recalled all his excellent comments, and Andersen, in particular, could remember many of them, which he now eagerly recounted, also those which everyone remembered as having annoyed Hans Brun, but now they were repeated with a double sense of irony, striking back at Paulsen, who was now perceived as the object of ridicule. And Ingebrigtsen became an expert at recounting the horror-inducing story about how Paulsen was unmasked. At first only through partial hints conveyed to the others seated at the table next to the wall on this particular side of Frederikke, but later telling the whole story to newcomers in their group and to students who just happened to sit down at their table. Ingebrigtsen's account got funnier and funnier, and more and more farcical, as he embroidered his description of how Paulsen kept wondering whether he would ever dare to take the first midterm in elementary mathematics in the fall. Ingebrigtsen's mimicry and gestures seemed priceless to his audience, especially the part of his story dealing with the arrival in Oslo of the sinister father, bent on fetching home his indebted son. At that point the original group, the newcomers, and any chance guests would all howl with laughter. But not everyone in the group laughed with equal heartiness. Hans Brun, for instance, might get mildly annoyed and interrupt Ingebrigtsen or the sneering Andersen as the latter recounted one of Paulsen's earlier remarks.

"Give Paulsen a rest," he might say.

Jan Brosten personally didn't like hearing about Paulsen either, at least not over and over, but he didn't say anything. Now and then Paul Buer might see him smile, and even on rare occasions laugh with abandon, but on the whole Paul noticed that Jan personally didn't care to hear the Paulsen stories.

Nor did Paul Buer like being reminded of Tor Erik Paulsen, but for him there was an additional reason. He felt a little stab of guilt whenever he heard the stories, and that was because he didn't really miss Paulsen. It was thanks to Paulsen that he had been admitted to this circle of science students. Yet even though Tor Erik Paulsen was the one who had introduced him to the others as a friend of his, Paul had never developed a close relationship with him; he had merely allowed himself to be ushered over to this table because, to be honest, he knew hardly anyone.

Later he felt closer to many others than he did to Paulsen, and by the time Paulsen was unmasked, he had actually become close friends with Jan Brosten.

Brosten was the genius of the group. They called him "A-Brosten" when he wasn't within earshot. The "A-" stood for the grade (1.1) that he usually received whenever he took an exam; and the two ones also symbolized the fact that he was number one at whatever he tried his hand, from the board game *couronne* to track and field events. He was the national champion in the 400-meter hurdles and also good at the 400-meter dash. As a university student he was in the process of completing his thesis in theoretical physics, and he'd been chosen to be a part-time teaching assistant for a renowned professor in the field, and of course a brilliant future was predicted for him, provided he didn't decide to switch fields and focus instead on astrophysics, which was something he occasionally hinted at doing. At that time our students, as well as our athletes, were frequently dubbed the flower of Norway's youth, and thus there is no reason why this *double-flower* shouldn't be presented as the flower of Norwegian youth here as well.

After a track and field meet or a national championship, it was especially nice for Norway's champion in the 400-meter hurdles to sit at the table with completely ordinary students, laughing at the jokes that were so diligently told, and shooting the breeze with that serious, almost indifferent expression of his. Many people thought Jan Brosten lived a totally different life outside this circle of friends, which was assumed to be merely peripheral to his real life. It was thought that he had an exciting life within the world of track and field, with championship banquets and admiring women inviting him to dance, or that he was constantly being invited to parties with younger intellectuals where conversations blazed and Jan was finally allowed to blossom. This was also the understanding among the group at the table. But it turned out not to be the case. This was his social life. This was his circle of acquaintances, it was around this table that he found his friends, and one of his best friends was the ordinary science student Paul Buer, whose friendship, symptomatically enough, began when Brosten helped Paul with a tricky math problem, enabling him to see the solution in all its clarity.

Jan Brosten did not put on airs. After his victory at the national championships in the 400-meter hurdles (a one-time occurrence), with some embarrassment he allowed the others at Blindern to congratulate him the next day, on a Monday, but he managed to stop one of them—it was Paulsen (before Paulsen was unmasked)—from getting everyone to sing "For He's a Jolly Good Fellow." Otherwise he enjoyed amusements and he was quick to laugh heartily at all sorts of jokes, perhaps especially at gags about mix-ups, but he wasn't good at telling jokes himself, or at least Paul Buer never heard him tell one. But Jan might, for instance, urge Ingebrigtsen (or Paulsen) to tell the one about the girl who didn't know, etc., etc. He didn't really say much, it was mostly small talk and brief remarks, usually about the weather, about the fact that Skeid had won the soccer match and Lightning had lost, and that today was Monday again. But when on rare occasion he did offer an opinion during a discussion, the others listened, because what he said was so well-conceived, so crystal clear, that it was impossible to contradict him. Yet his words were mere generalities. Readily accepted opinions. For instance, that it's healthy for democracy when the conservatives and the socialists take turns holding power. That it was healthy for the party that had previously been in power and lost it, and for the party which had previously been the opposition but now took the reins of government. Democracy would crumble if government didn't change hands occasionally, in accordance with democratic elections. This sounded so convincingly sensible that the students who had voted conservative in the election realized they shouldn't be cheering too loudly, because the election results were first and foremost a victory for democracy, and that wasn't something to gloat about. Or vice versa (depending on the actual election results).

It was this sort of argument that Jan Brosten might occasionally voice. Aside from the great clarity of his thoughts, what was most striking was the fact that he didn't seem particularly enamored of what he said. He actually seemed indifferent whenever he put forth these carefully conceived arguments of his. Sounding a little weary, as if he personally didn't think there was anything special to discuss, but since they happened to be talking about this particular topic, and since he had so thoroughly considered the matter, then this was his opinion. Yet, in spite of everything, he had spent a large part of his life in situations which necessitated that what he talked about also affected his own life, so he must have had a serious relationship to these thoughts of his. After all, he had carefully considered these ideas, such as the importance of regime changes in a democracy, and most likely he would have been infuriated if anyone had challenged him.

Jan Brosten and Paul Buer played chess together, privately,

in Paul's room in the student dorms in Sogn. Jan often went home with Paul after classes were over at the university, and they would play chess, usually two games, until late at night. Sometimes Jan would show up at the dorms unannounced and ask whether they could have a game. He didn't live in the dorms but rather with an aunt on Hegdehaugsveien. Paul had never been there; he didn't think Jan ever invited anyone home to his aunt's place, so he didn't even know exactly where on Hegdehaugsveien she lived. Maybe it was because he lived with his aunt that Jan liked to go out to the dorms in Sogn, maybe it was one way for him to take part in student life, maybe he experienced there a freedom that you can't have when living in the maid's room in the home of your mother's sister while you're studying at the university in Oslo. At any rate, Jan seemed to thrive when taking part for a brief time in the dorm life in Sogn.

So Jan Brosten and Paul Buer played chess together. They were an odd pair, especially since Jan was a much better player than Paul. If Jan had focused his attention on chess by joining a chess club, he probably would have gone far; the same could not be said of Paul. Yet both were happy amateurs, except that Jan was a much better player. What we can say is that Jan almost always won, and when he didn't, it was a stalemate. Once in a while Paul would fight his way to a stalemate, and he was proud of that. And let's be honest, sometimes Paul did win, on occasions when Jan had squandered most of his pieces in a battle with his own fascinating intuition. Because Jan played in a way that was directly contrary to how many would have thought he'd proceed. He opened with great daring, what many might call a foolhardy opening, and took chances; it seemed as if he were moving randomly and taking a certain pleasure in doing so. But gradually a plan would materialize in his mind, which he would then, but only then, follow mercilessly, yet the whole time making use of diversionary maneuvers to mislead his opponent. Only when his opponent, i.e., Paul, had no possibility of evading what was bound to come—checkmate—did this plan become apparent. Now and then it might seem as if Paul had the upper hand in the game, at least on those occasions when Jan's too bold and unorthodox openings had led to certain serious losses, for instance squandering a knight in exchange for nothing, but that was actually not the case, and Paul knew it, because he never (or almost never) won; the best he could do was to fight hard for a stalemate.

Considering that Jan Brosten was such a brilliant person, he made a strikingly bland impression. This blandness was also much in evidence when he rang the bell at Paul Buer's dorm in Sogn, and Paul let him in, and he dumped his bag of workout clothes in the shared entryway, since he was coming straight from a practice for the 400-meter hurdles at the field of the new sports college in Kringsjå, and he asked, perhaps with a slightly expectant smile, whether they could play a game of chess. But the smile quickly disappeared as soon as he set up the board and began his brash and risky opening moves, after which he concealed his covertly deliberate plan. It ought to be possible to compare his way of playing chess with his general, readily acceptable attitudes toward "reality," in order to understand, or at least to be astounded by, the difference, as well as the astonishing and perhaps also crystal clear perspectives to which his chess game pointed, considering that what he expressed through chess was just as much in his capacity as an amateur as the opinions and convictions he espoused about society and daily life in Norway during his student years; and you have to assume that his way of playing chess was more in line with his serious, impassioned work as a gifted student and professor's assistant in theoretical physics than with his opinions about "reality," seeing as there was an almost incomprehensibly vast leap from one activity (as a professor's assistant in theoretical physics) to the other (his opinions).

As a chess player he could accept losing, in fact it might seem as if he possessed a certain inner drive that challenged him to end up in the losing position. When on rare occasion he did lose, he behaved like a proper loser, meaning slightly pissed off, which is how a winner wants a loser to behave so that he can bask in the fruits of his victory. He took risks, real risks, which he actually seemed to enjoy taking within the parameters of the game. Yet he also thought deeply, pondering countermoves well in advance without revealing his intentions, trying to put up a smoke screen via misleading moves that would make his opponent sense danger from a completely different direction on the board than where it was actually coming from. But when he expressed himself in such excellent Norwegian regarding "reality," as a young Norwegian citizen, a promising student, a flower, he had undoubtedly carefully considered what he chose to say; to call these thoughts of a risky nature would be utterly wrong. When he spoke of "reality," he had no tolerance for losing; in that instance he disliked taking risks or making any of the sort of great leaps in his thought processes that bore a similarity to the way he conducted his deliberate onslaught toward a spot on the chessboard where his opponent, unaware, would end up fettered for good and which, when the other player had understood his moves and seen where they led, he actually experienced as a demonstration of freedom. When he spoke of "reality," none of this occurred. He might be both critical and skeptical but not "free" in his thoughts even though he, as the good Norwegian he was, chose freedom as his starting point whenever he judged a phenomenon, and it was on the basis of freedom that he either supported or condemned a particular phenomenon.

It's possible that, if presented with the problem, Jan Brosten himself might have claimed that the way he thought of "reality" was more in keeping with his scientific ingress into the spheres of theoretical physics than with the rash way he played chess, and the approach he used to express his ideas about "reality," and regarding scientific encroachment, retained an adherence to the small, trivial principles upon which both a societal judgment and a scientific judgment (or formula) rely, something that cannot be ignored without disastrous results. In that case, we have to view his chess game as an uninhibited and time-constrained surrender to both his own and many others' yearning for the intoxicating sense of freedom that is the very essence of gambling.

In that case, the astonishing and almost incomprehensible difference in perspectives exists exclusively on an aesthetic level. You'd have to be someone who shared Jan Brosten's opinions to a fanatical degree in order to assert that his societal ideas, in spite of their admirable clarity, were particularly "beautiful," but few, if any, would deny that a mathematical formula used in theoretical physics can in fact be unbelievably beautiful. For an outsider it might be difficult to accept that something extremely attractive and something rather plain might have the same source and be fundamentally two aspects of the same thing.

On the other hand, it's easy to focus on the unnecessary gamble involved in Jan Brosten's opening moves, which obviously gave him a great deal of satisfaction, especially because they were unnecessary and served no purpose. He would actually have been a much better chess player without this tendency. But he chose, with open eyes, to weaken his position as a player in this way. Why? Sometimes this "why?" also occurred to his opponent, Paul Buer, in a flash of insight. At those moments he might feel a certain embarrassment, and once, on one of those rare occasions when he'd actually won the game, he said, after the initial giddy pride at having won subsided, that he wouldn't have won if Jan Brosten had played with the intention of beating him.

Jan was clearly upset, Paul could see that, but he quickly recovered and replied: "How typical of you, Paul, to think that way."

Paul shrugged, still feeling a bit embarrassed, and suggested they go to the kitchen (which he shared with three other students, all of whom had rooms that opened onto it), and fry some eggs as a victory celebration, the way they always did, no matter who won the game. So that's what they did. They sat down at the kitchen table. Paul fried four eggs, and Jan buttered several thick slices of bread. Then they sat there and wolfed down the food, youthfully minded, in a way, in the late 1960s, perhaps while the sports bag of the previous year's Norwegian champion in the 400-meter hurdles lay in a corner where it had been tossed.

Jan Brosten also took Paul Buer to the gymnasium in Velferdsbygget in Blindern, where they joined a bunch of guys playing handball. Several of the others from the group who sat at the table in Frederikke were there too, brought in by the quiet and serious Jan Brosten. Andersen and Per Arne Pedersen were there. As well as a guy named Gloer. They played one or two afternoons a week. For Jan, this was a great diversion from his real training as a track-and-field athlete. Paul was the goalkeeper; growing up he'd been a soccer goalie, and now he was the handball goalie. What he liked least about being a handball goalie was the fact that the ball was so fucking hard that it stung his fingertips, or the palms of his hands, whenever he made a save or blocked a shot, to say nothing of how much it hurt to get one in the face. It had been quite different to be a soccer goalie, and he recalled with nostalgia the round form and soft leather of a soccer ball. The handball was also round, but the hard leather covering the compact and diminutive ball made any attempt to regard the ball as really round impossible. Yet by playing handball Paul became a member of OSAA, which stood for the Oslo Student Athletic Association, and it meant that on Saturdays, along with a bunch of like-minded cohorts, after the lectures were over and the reading rooms were closed, around two or three o'clock, he would head up to Nordmarka to the OSAA cabin, hiking in the fall and skiing there in the winter. In winter they would spend the night, ski all day Sunday, and then return to the OSAA cabin to pack up their rucksacks and sleeping bags to return to the city, where some of them would go out and eat dinner together at one of Oslo's "better restaurants," as they called it (rather misleadingly, it should be noted).

It was at the OSAA cabin that the ladies awaited. Actually, most of them waited first at Majorstua, where they met on the platform, took the tram up to Frognerseteren, and from there headed to the cabin, on skis in the wintertime. Some were the steady girlfriends of guys in the group, and they might bring along their dearest friends. Because some in the group had actually acquired steady girlfriends, such as Pedersen and the guy named Gloer. But most of them had not, not at that time, and for that reason they set off, on skis, for the OSAA cabin, where the ladies awaited. No one knew where they came from, but they had some sort of association with OSAA, most were university students, at any rate, or nursing students who knew someone who was a member of OSAA. But we have to assume that Jan Brosten went there because it was simply a fine means of relaxation, and maybe Paul Buer felt the same way. Maybe Andersen too. It definitely was a fine means of relaxation to find themselves, after long days of studying, out in the white forest of Nordmarka, on skis, in the midst, or even at the very back of a group of friends, moving in a long line, cross-country through Nordmarka, along trails and over hills, down flat stretches, at dusk, which turned to pitch dark before they even reached the OSAA cabin.

And there the ladies were waiting. Now those serious-minded and extremely ordinary students of science, who were so happy to play handball twice a week, met the ladies. "The opposite sex," which they undoubtedly called the weaker sex, at least that's what they all said out loud; though for them it was also the opposite sex they were now meeting, and they may have been looking forward to this moment all week. A charged atmosphere was brewing, that cannot be denied, and Paul Buer felt shy. Only the fewest of these science students—who played handball twice a week and who went up to the OSAA cabin on weekends—were or considered themselves any kind of Don Juan. And most would have silently agreed if anyone told them they weren't especially good-looking, though they would have defiantly and in most cases truthfully added that they weren't particularly distinctive in terms of the other end of the spectrum either. But the atmosphere had become so strangely charged. Everyone pretended to ignore it, but everything had changed. Eroticism had entered the picture, but evidently in a nonerotic sort of way. They became competitors. Even though each of them individually concluded that there wasn't much competition, they were indeed competing for the favor of the lovely ladies. Each offered himself to the opposite sex, not directly, not as a seducer, but they did offer themselves in a general sense.

It was striking how sociable these taciturn and reserved science students actually were when it came right down to it. When in the presence of ladies. They made a point of not behaving in an affected manner. They made a point of being themselves, even when they weren't talking but merely listening and laughing at what someone else had said. It was through their own inner resources that they sought happiness, even when they kept in the background and only their contented laughter revealed that they were glad to be there. They offered their sense of confidence, their lighthearted temperament, and their self-assurance. Their firm shoulders and the silent crooks of their arms, you might say. Quite unlike the way they behaved at the table in Frederikke where each sat in splendid isolation with his Andersen-ness, his Brosten-ness, and his Gloer-ness (even his Buer-ness, you might say, although no, not here, not now, Paul is shy, he watches the whole scene from outside and hardly manages to say a word, he feels sick whenever, for some reason, he has to get up and walk across the floor in his thick wool socks). They showed off. Quite openly, they showed off, in a perfectly ordinary context. A cabin weekend. Sitting in front of the fireplace. Sitting around the table. Good stories. Quiet conversations. They showed off with all their might. Chopping wood. Carrying wood. Lighting a fire in the fireplace. Displaying a pleasant charm. Carving a leg of mutton with a sheath knife and handing slices to the girl sitting closest. A humorous glint in their eyes. They all acted so strangely self-confident. Not for a second did it look as if they were desperately searching for happiness.

"Desperately searching for happiness." You could have tried out this statement on them, and you would have been met with indulgence, at best. Shouldn't a person be allowed to spend a weekend up at the student cabin without "desperately searching for happiness?" Who said that? Would he mind repeating it? But no one would have volunteered. So it might as well have not been said at all. Good heavens, a person should be allowed to get acquainted with a sweet member of the opposite sex without "desperately searching for happiness."

And maybe they were not desperately searching for happiness. Even Paul Buer was probably not. Although he might have been the one to say those unfortunate words about all of them if he hadn't known what a poor reception the words would have provoked. But above all else, Paul Buer felt shy about what he was seeing. And about the game itself. The fact that they were showing off. And why was he shy? Well, because he had nothing to show off. He didn't have confident shoulders or arm crooks to offer one of those creatures who were present in the same room with him. Paul felt invaded, now as always, by the insidiousness of existence, and he wished he could escape from that room where the charged erotic atmosphere was surfacing, in looks of the eye, gestures of the hand, and strange innuendos laden with promises for the recipient. And Jan Brosten, can it really be said that he was "desperately searching for happiness?" If so, all he had to do was hold out his hand, because there it was, the happiness that he was supposedly so desperately searching for. Because the female eyes were turned toward Jan Brosten, they were almost all looking at him, though he hardly noticed. (No, he did notice; whenever Jan and Paul shared a meal in Paul's student lodgings, after having played chess, they sometimes started talking about women they knew from the OSAA cabin who had come on to Jan by staring at him adoringly, usually with their chin resting on their hand, which was supported in turn by a slender elbow. Jan often talked about them to Paul, discussing them and recounting what sort of impression they had made on him. Visual impressions, both good and bad. Good qualities that were immediately apparent, as well as less-good qualities that were immediately apparent. He might say that he liked the way a particular girl walked. Her "gait," as Jan Brosten called it. But he might also mention her voice, which in the long run could seem a little too pushy.)

"The voice is important, Paul," said Jan. "If you're really going to enter into a relationship, you'll be hearing that voice for the rest of your life, in all sorts of situations, also when times are hard. Because life will have many hard times to offer; we might forget about that now, when life seems as easy as it does, when everything seems to open before us," said Jan. So Jan Brosten did not call attention to himself, he didn't put himself out there. Only a few times did Paul ever see him get involved, slightly, ever so slightly, with a member of the opposite sex, until he met the one whom he would end up marrying. Once Paul was on the tram on his way back from Frognerseteren on a wintry Sunday afternoon. In the middle of the tram crowded with Sunday tourists going home, he saw Jan twining fingers with a girl he'd spent a lot of time talking to the night before; he'd also skied next to her almost all day long on that Sunday.

And Per Arne Pedersen, was he "desperately searching for happiness" before he met the girl he was now going steady with? Yes, Pedersen had put himself out there, that was definitely true, with all the solidity that a future biology teacher in secondary school could offer, and he'd found success very quickly, maybe because he also liked to compete in that way; by then he'd achieved an air of narcissistic authority, which had greatly appealed to the ladies, astonishing though this was to those who knew Pedersen only from Frederikke and Blindern. And now he had a steady girlfriend whom he mostly saw only on weekends. Here, at the OSAA cabin. They would spend the night in a separate room, or else they would share a room with another couple in a similar situation. The others, those who didn't have steady dates, slept on the floor in front of the fireplace in sleeping bags arranged haphazardly, both the men and the women. So it had to be to those gentlemen on the floor, in their sleeping bags, that you'd have to turn in order to find someone who was "desperately searching for happiness." Andersen, for example. Andersen who, at the OSAA cabin, was the embodiment of helpfulness. He was the one who chopped wood, carried wood, lit the fire, waxed the ladies' skis, or advised them on how to wax their skis; he walked around grinning, that ungainly person, who had an indefinable touch of Andersen-ness about him, and many of the young females clearly didn't really know what to make of him. Was he "desperately searching for happiness?"

No, he was perfectly calm. There was something utterly "typical Andersen" about him. He was waiting, patiently, like the others. In an erotic atmosphere in which all the insidiousness of existence was completely lacking except internally, and kept well hidden among a few individuals who were present. It was the eternal game that was unfolding in that totally distinctive and Norwegian setting. A timbered cabin in Nordmarka. Outside, the soughing of the dense spruce trees in the nighttime wind. Inside, healthy Norwegian students of both sexes. On the lookout for a mate for life. Nothing less. This lent the whole scene a serious note, and caused it to be mistakenly characterized as "a desperate search for happiness." Because they were all waiting for destiny to strike them, or smile on them. Waiting for something to happen. Each was waiting to find his life partner. Was she here? Tonight? Was Andersen waiting for his life partner? Was she here? Would she really be here? Could that really be true? If so, she would have to give him a sign, a gesture, hold out her hand toward him, Andersen, in such a way that he could understand and begin to hope: a glance, a gesture, a sudden candor, or an attention-grabbing modesty in a lowered gaze, directed toward him, in this case Andersen, who is here, fully present in his Andersen-form, which she as yet does not know, so that as yet it arouses no response from her. His Andersen-ness, which she hasn't yet seen or associated with anything, arouses no response. On any given evening Andersen may have looked for many such signs, from so many different girls, but perhaps he found none that gave him anything more than false hopes, like in the morning, when they were heading out for the daylong skiing expedition, which had little likelihood of providing more than a minor disappointment, a crushed hope, a glance that wasn't interested, merely scrutinizing and then politely rejecting; that's what you'd see when the day brightened, when you had to wax your own skis and the eternal game continued, now under changed external circumstances, signifying that there was nothing special about the fact that Andersen was waxing her skis, of course he should be free to wax her skis, but don't think that's anything important, that's what her cold shoulder would be saying.

But before that, a long night spent in the sleeping bag on the floor here in the OSAA cabin. Because of the skiing planned for the next day, they would all go to bed shortly after midnight. Those who had steady dates disappeared into their own rooms, and those without steady dates got out their sleeping bags and unrolled them. An eventful evening was over! They crawled inside their sleeping bags, but nobody could sleep. They lay there, thinking and speculating, and wondering about their prospects for the following day and which signs from the evening might possibly be interpreted as hopes for the morning and the long ski expedition, filled with possible developments that might ensue. But then the silence was broken. A man's voice broke through, uttering a salient remark that had just occurred to him and that someone lying there in a sleeping bag on the floor might appreciate, a remark that might, as she lay there in the dark, stir a sense of admiration for the one who had spoken. This remark was then instantly countered with another, and then a third, as someone told a joke he should have told long ago, before a fourth person, in the dark, decided to praise to the skies the present day and age. The fourth male voice inquired enthusiastically whether they had noticed the moon's hazy passage across the celestial vault that night. And whether they, like him, had felt a pride and a quivering sense of anticipation at the thought that the day was fast approaching when a spacecraft would land on the moon, and the first human would climb out, wearing a remarkable spacesuit, and hesitantly plant the first human foot on that strange orb, and from there, in a state of near weightlessness, peer into space, and way far away, in the dark sky, see our own planet making its hazy passage across the celestial vault. He also asked us to think further, and not least about the starry expanse above us that night. To think about the miracle that soon we ourselves would be out there, among the stars, in a spaceship on our way to the planet Mars. In twenty years, before we turned fifty, we'd be there, on the planet Mars, and we'd finally find out whether there was other life in our solar system. This would happen in our lifetime, he solemnly pronounced in the dark where the students of both sexes lay in sleeping bags, listening. A fifth person was so strongly affected by all this that he began to speak in order to change the subject to something else entirely, mentioning the microscopic universe here on earth. He talked about the computer-created brain, which would provoke a revolution surpassing everything else. About space travel and stellar research. He predicted that the human brain was capable of constructing a robot brain that could think independently, all on its own, and surpass the most brilliant of human brains, what we call human genius, and actually put it in its place. He even took the liberty of being specific enough to predict that in twenty years, this type of computer would be capable of beating the world champion in chess, and winning not just once, not just twice, not just five or even six out of ten games, but *all ten games*, delivering such a devastating defeat that humanity would have to pronounce a computer as the new world champion in chess; that's what the fifth male proclaimed there in the dark, speaking in a sonorous voice. But then they heard a sixth voice, and it was Jan Brosten. He said this might well be possible, but it all depended on who was the reigning world chess champion at the time. Some individuals became the world champion because they played in a supremely methodical way, which made their game systematically superior. If the computer faced that type of world champion, the machine might well win, and no doubt, sooner or later, a computer would be developed which such a world champion would never be able to beat. Yet there was another type of chess player, and some individuals of this type also became world champions. They were the intuitive players. Faced with such a world champion, the victory would never be a sure thing. An intuitive world champion in chess would never be the predicted loser, even when playing the most advanced of computers. That's what Jan Brosten said from deep inside his sleeping bag. The others waited in suspense to hear what the fifth male voice would reply, but when he eventually did respond it was to agree with Jan Brosten. This led to a brief pause for quiet contemplation, during which everyone silently expressed tremendous gratitude for the intuitive intelligence of human beings, which meant that under no circumstances was defeat a foregone conclusion; but then an enthusiastic seventh male voice burst out of the darkness to add his praise for the present day and age. The seventh voice spoke with elation, almost feverishly, about what he called the Norwegian oil venture. He based his remarks on the vast, valuable resources that lay hidden in the sea off Norway's weather-beaten coast, resources which modern technology most likely would now be able to raise to the light of day as fuel for the real world, with its infinite number of spinning wheels. In other words, he was talking about the search for oil, which at that time had started on Norway's continental shelf, and about the future. The person speaking asked the others to picture for themselves the great miracle occurring in the North Sea at that very moment, even on that very night. The search for commercially exploitable deposits of black gold would change Norway. He asked all of them to picture the castle in the air that had taken the form of gigantic drilling platforms out there in the North Sea.

Though they might not use these exact words, the students nevertheless shared his poetic fervor as they added their tributes to their own day and age with all its enormous possibilities. Lying in their separate sleeping bags in the dark, they fantasized out loud, and others hearing their words would add their own comments. But there was something peculiar about this poetic fervor from these young men, who were all students of science. Actually, there should be nothing strange about like-minded students with a certain knowledge of mathematics and physics admiring and praising technological achievements made in our day and age, along with others they know would occur in the future. This was an invocation. And they knew what they were invoking, they were very familiar with such things, but why invoke them? And why here? They would never have talked this way at Frederikke or Blindern. Of course they admired their own day and age, and they also found it exciting to be living in an era that offered such enormous opportunities and allowed for such formidable changes in the way human beings would live and think, but they preferred to keep a safe distance. They didn't want to be in the middle of the upheaval, with its dynamic exertion of power, but preferred instead to read about it in the newspapers, or see images of it unfolding on TV, so they could then nod, impressed and approving. Fully understanding. For this they had adopted a specific type of language at Frederikke and Blindern, a language they spoke daily. But out here, in the OSAA cabin in Nordmarka, their voices radiated a manly and poetic fervor when they flung their words into the dark. Because here they were flinging their words toward the opposite sex, the girls who lay quietly in their sleeping bags in the same room. The ones they were trying to seduce. Not with themselves but with the era to which they belonged. The age of oil. They were seducing with the age of oil, which at that time took up very little room in the general consciousness of these members of

the opposite sex. It was these young men's own secure crook of
the arm describing the oil venture, which *they* understood, and
they were among the first. The space age. The space age and a
life partner. Their children would grow up in the midst of the
space age. The information age. Computers.

Listen here, woman, an ordinary person will rejoice at the
emergence of the information age. We do too. Students in the
mid-twentieth century. Hear our manly voices on this night before the skiing expedition tomorrow through the white landscape! My dear, the ordinary person lying here awake and con-
templative can offer an extraordinary future, if you don't turn
up your nose. This withdrawn and taciturn student here, my
dear, invites you on an exciting journey through life, venturing
into the unknown.

Oh yes, they presented one invitation after another. They offered the modernity they had already fundamentally rejected,
at least as lodestars for their own lives. The boring math teachers of the future shone as if they were its vital oil executives,
with the whole world as their field of action because they were
bathed in a desire to find a potential life partner. They were fully
engaged in justifying themselves, and their own entrance into
adult life. They lay there in their sleeping bags, understanding
their own day and age as they listened and waited for a sign
from a potential life partner, who also lay there in the dark and
listened, presumably with admiration for everything that was
being said. That was why the male students were aroused whenever a female voice occasionally broke in, not to participate in
the discussion or to add her praise, but instead to offer a slightly
impertinent remark. This impertinent comment intoxicated

them all, egging them on in their nocturnal praise of the age in which they were living.

Paul Buer was also there. He lay in his sleeping bag, listening somewhat distractedly and drowsily to everything being said. Actually, he was lost in his own thoughts, preoccupied with a sudden idea that had occurred to him, surprising him and making him happy. But he was also listening to the words the other students were flinging into the dark. He listened to the tributes to the Space Age. To the computers created by human brains that would soon put humans in their place. Although not in areas involving intuitive intelligence, where under no circumstances could humans be considered the guaranteed losers. He listened to the voice talking about the oil venture in the North Sea. He listened and listened, and not without pleasure. But did he really hear what they were saying? Did that voice—and by the way, it was Ingebrigtsen who was speaking—imply that they were supposed to imagine what was going on in the North Sea? That couldn't be right. And suddenly Paul heard, to his surprise, his own voice resounding in the room, and he heard himself say that it wasn't *in* the North Sea that oil might eventually be found, but rather *under* the North Sea, beneath the bottom of the North Sea. That's where the oil was, hopefully in commercially exploitable quantities. So it's *under* the North Sea, not *in* the sea, Paul Buer triumphantly announced in the dark of night to those students, of both sexes, lying in their sleeping bags. A silence ensued after he spoke, followed by an annoyed outburst from others in their sleeping bags. Not only from Ingebrigtsen; many other voices also exclaimed that there was no use getting hung up on such trivial matters. What a pedant they had among them! What a nitpicker, they cried into the dark as they tossed and turned in their sleeping bags (thought Paul). But then Jan Brosten's voice broke in to support his friend Paul Buer. Jan said that it was true enough that the search for oil was taking place within a specific geographic area *in* the North Sea, but what they were looking for was actually *under* the North Sea. When talking about the search for oil in the North Sea, you consequently had to talk about the search in a geographical sense. If you said that the search for oil is taking place *under* the North Sea, you'd be saying where it was occurring from a geographical perspective and you'd also be making a concrete comment about the nature of the search. This was therefore a better means of expression, because it also enriched the imagination in a true way. There was no oil in the North Sea, damn it; everyone in this room knew that, even the guy who said there was.

After this, the conversation faded. No one made any attempt to revive it, because it was late at night, and the next day awaited them. Sleep made its way among the ranks of students of both sexes, and soon they were all sound asleep. Except for Paul Buer. Paul couldn't sleep. Not because he was the one who had punctured the enthusiastic homage to the present day and age and turned several of the male students against him; he felt a hint of regret, but no more than that. No, he lay there thinking about something else entirely. He was wide awake after making his own big decision. At the age of twenty-three, he had decided what he wanted to be. He had decided to make use of his science studies to become a meteorologist. I'm going to be a meteorologist, he thought, solemnly, as he savored these words, which he'd never voiced before. He felt a great sense of satisfaction in his whole body. He didn't think: I can become a meteorologist, or I wonder whether I will become a meteorologist; instead he thought, spontaneously and with a strong certainty in his body: I'm going to be a meteorologist. Me. A meteorologist.

Paul Buer had made up his mind. Lying in his sleeping bag on the floor of the OSAA cabin, surrounded by sleeping students of both sexes, he was wide awake and trembling with joy at finally having made his big decision. He would become a meteorologist. He had long realized that he wanted to do something useful, this was a life-affirming requirement that would govern his life, and now he finally knew in what way he would be a useful citizen of society. In his capacity as a meteorologist. As someone who could, based on countless observations, figure out what the weather would be, even before it became what was forecast, and in that way he would contribute to one of humanity's genuine triumphs: control of the violent and insane forces of nature by making use of the laws to which they are subject, in spite of everything, and surprisingly enough. In this way it was possible to get a jump on the forces of nature, avoiding them, finding safety, and then waiting. This was no small decision for a young man of twenty-three. He'd been weighing the matter for months. Cautiously he had hinted at it to Jan, who had supported him, but he'd still had his doubts. The consequences of making such a choice were enormous. When you decided to become something, that was what you became forever, there was no way back, no possibility of changing your mind, at least not in a practical sense, unless you were willing to admit defeat, acknowledging that you just weren't good enough after all. Paul

Buer had now decided that he was good enough. It was joy that kept him awake all night, almost until dawn.

For that reason he didn't feel groggy with sleep at any time the next day; not at breakfast, while waxing his skis, or on the long expedition that the young students took through Nordmarka, or on the equally long, if not longer, return to the cabin, through the wintry white world. Nor while they were packing and cleaning up, or while skiing back to the tram stop at Frognerseteren, or on the tram ride back down to the Oslo basin in the afternoon. At Majorstua he said goodbye to the others. Some were going to a restaurant to eat dinner together. But not Paul Buer, because he was meeting Armand.

Paul and Armand had kept in touch, but they seldom saw each other. Yet a few days ago, Armand had phoned and suggested they see a movie together on Sunday. At the Gimle theater. A film by the French director Godard. They were supposed to meet outside the Gimle just before seven o'clock. Paul arrived late because he'd made a quick stop at his dorm in Sogn to drop off his skis and change his clothes, but Armand had already bought two tickets. They went inside the theater. The lights went out at once, and the film started. It was a strange one. Afterward, as they walked from the theater to a restaurant called the Krølle on Uranienborgveien, a good distance away, but neither of them knew of any place closer where they could get a beer, Armand asked Paul what he thought of the movie.

"Hmm, well, there was some action here and there, maybe even too much, because it was kind of confusing. But that's better than those movies with no action at all. Remember that one with the geometric park and the castle where they put on

Rosmersholm? There was no action at all in that one," he added.

Armand laughed. "*Rosmer*, not *Rosmersholm*. So you still remember *Last Year at Marienbad*? See that? It's not so easy to stop thinking about epoch-making art. The same holds for this one. I thought it was great. I've seen it a total of three times."

"Uh-huh, it was kind of strange, the guy who painted his face blue before he fired off the charge. I guess we were supposed to laugh, right?" said Paul a bit cautiously.

"You can laugh whenever you like," replied Armand.

They were now sitting in the Krølle, and each had a beer. Paul wondered whether he should tell Armand about the big decision he'd made. He really wanted to, because if he did, he would be presenting himself to his old childhood friend as a completely new and changed person. But the decision was still too new, he didn't feel ready to tell anyone else yet. He'd talked to Jan Brosten several times over the course of the day during the ski expedition in Nordmarka, but he hadn't mentioned his decision to him either. So even though he now felt a great urge to tell Armand—and specifically him because they'd known each other for so long, from when they were kids and through their school years, they had gone to secondary school together and stayed friends through thick and thin, and then gone to Oslo to attend the university—Paul still hesitated. Instead, he talked about the weekend trips to the OSAA cabin. Way up in Nordmarka. He described the setting, what they did there, etc., etc., and not hiding the fact that lots of ladies were present.

"Sometimes I wonder, most recently I wondered late last night, whether all of us there are desperately searching for happiness. Do you think that's what we're doing, Armand?"

Armand looked up from his beer glass and smiled. "Yes, I really think you are. There can be no doubt about it," he said, laughing. "But I am too," he added. "Desperately searching for happiness," he said with a sigh.

————

8. Here I must point out that N, who appears at this stage in the novel, and who plays the role of an utterly decisive woman in Armand's life, is not included *here*, in the footnotes, at the same time. Here we find her twin sister. Her twin sister with whom Armand had a strange Easter escapade, and who he later sometimes claims is the mother of his daughter, whom N bore him. Here in the footnotes N is almost erased from his circle of friends, and Armand's desire—here we are talking about the twin sister, and even though N's voice is almost identical to her twin sister's (they're almost impossible to distinguish except by those who are very close to the two of them, and even in that case it would only be a hint, a qualified guess, that he, she, or they could tell the voices apart, a mere possibility) it's the twin sister's voice we hear now—and Armand's delight at hearing the sound from her vocal cords is not delight at hearing the sound from N's vocal cords, but hearing the sound from the twin sister's vocal cords. And yet, even though N is absent from this footnote, here, at this point in time, her shadow looms over it, or rather, over the twin sister, without the twin sister's shadow looming over, or anywhere near N, in the novel over there, at this point in time. There it is N who is clear, as clear as can be, considering the literary circumstances, while here N is invisible. The only mention of N here is in the previous

footnote, in Paul Buer's version of his university years, where Armand was a secondary character, and where Paul Buer expressed his puzzled amazement over the fact that every time he visited Armand at the Frederikke student cafeteria in Blindern, he was always surrounded by beautiful women. There is reason to assume that what Paul Buer observed was Armand surrounded by N and her twin sister, and possibly a few of their friends who might alternate but were always beautiful. N was studying French, and her twin sister art history, precisely during that semester, which must have been the spring semester of 1967, while during the fall semester of 1967 it was the opposite, N was studying art history and her twin sister French, and their various girlfriends were almost as beautiful as they were, so that Armand at that time was always surrounded at the table by a bevy of beautiful female students—the twin sisters and their friends—and since there were two of them, they had many friends. (I should probably mention that there were also young men in this group.)

One morning, two weeks before Easter, one of the twins came alone to the table where Armand was sitting and took a seat. A half hour later one of her, or N's, girlfriends arrived and sat down, but during the brief half hour that they'd been alone, the twin sister had given Armand an invitation. The result of this was that ten days later Armand was sitting in the night train to Bergen, traveling over the mountains of Vestland, or Western Norway, as he spent a sleepless night in one of the cars that was not a sleeping car, but was equipped with those adjustable seats that allow a person to drowse but never really sleep. Early in the morning he arrived in Bergen and walked through the empty streets down to Vågen harbor, where he boarded a ferry to one of the towns north of there, situated all the way out by the ocean, where the waves of the Atlantic roll in toward the Norwegian coast. The ferry ride took all day, and it was dark by the time he reached the little coastal town where the twin sister had grown up. He went ashore and wandered through the deserted streets that were meagerly illuminated by streetlights and the glow from shop windows, as he searched for a small one-and-a-half-story house that was supposed to be at the end of a cul-de-sac whose name he had jotted down in his notebook. The town was strangely windswept, and smelled of wind and the sea. The harbor lay protected behind a breakwater. There was a church spire. A mechanic's workshop. Screeching gulls and the smell of fish guts. A market square, police station, and fire station. All of it facing the ocean. As Armand searched for the house at the end of a specific cul-de-sac it occurs to me that I've been here before. During the whole trip, from the moment Armand took his seat on the night train to Bergen, I had an inkling of where this journey would lead, a hunch that evolved into certainty when he boarded the ferry and began the trip across the waters of the Vestland archipelago. It's true that I have never actually seen the islands with my own eyes, but I have a clear image of them in my mind's eye, even of the town where Armand went ashore after spending the whole day on this little ferry with all the stops it made. The whole town, including the trip there, seemed to be clipped from an interrupted dream I'd had, and after a few days I recalled where this déjà vu was from. It wasn't from a dream, but from my own literary landscape. Once, many years ago, one of my protagonists was supposed to vanish from his own novel and end up in this town. He was supposed to go underground, disappear, and reemerge in this town with a new identity. Unfortunately I never finished this conceit because the novel ended before I got that far. It was completed in the sense that I had nothing more to add to what I'd already put down on the page in black and white, so this idea of a new identity in the unfamiliar little coastal town in Vestland must have either been realized somehow in the novel, or when it came right down to it, could not be inserted into it. But now this town has popped up again, twenty years later, in a different novel, recounting an episode that supposedly took place around 1970, that is, over thirty-five years ago. I have to ask: Why does this town pop up now, fifteen years before it appeared in my literary landscape for the first time? There is no parallel between the young Armand V. of around 1970 and the protagonist from the novel I wrote fifteen years later. Armand did not pop up here in order to switch identities; on the contrary he received an ambiguous invitation, which might involve one of the great adventures of his young life. He did not know this little coastal town in Vestland, he had traveled here in response to a challenge, and in all haste. Maybe he'd had other plans for Easter that he'd canceled, or avoided, in favor of this journey.

Armand walked around in this unfamiliar little town by the Atlantic, searching for a little one-and-a-half-story house that was supposed to be at the end of a cul-de-sac whose name he had written in his notebook. The town was almost deserted, but some young people were hanging out at a hotdog stand, as they did in every isolated small town in Norway, at least in 1970. He could have asked them for directions but didn't, because he didn't want to draw attention, even though he hadn't been instructed not to do so. He continued searching on his own, walking up one street and down another, seeking out short cul-de-sacs, which he then explored until he came to their farthest point, where there was often a house; but not until the fifth try did he find the right cul-de-sac, and since this house was also one-and-a-half-story, and small, he went up the stone steps and rang the bell. The door was opened by a man about Armand's own age, who let him in. Inside the house a woman with a baby awaited him; this was obviously a young couple with a baby who would let him stay the night in anticipation of the twin sister's arrival. He was shown to his own room, a small one that could be locked from the inside. The couple served him dinner and wine and asked him how the trip had been. Later that evening another couple showed up with a guitar, more wine was set on the table, and the two young men played guitar, the two young women sang, and Armand joined in on the chorus. But the twin sister did not show up.

The next day Armand did not go out, but stayed inside with a book he had brought along in case he had time to study. His hosts kept to themselves. The weather was splendid, spring-time with an intense blue sky, and the young couple went for a long walk with the baby buggy. Armand opened a window in the living room and watched them cross the little cul-de-sac that opened onto one of the town's main streets. He noticed that there was a cold wind outside, colder than it seemed when he had opened the window and looked out, so he shut it again. When his hosts returned, they made lunch, and Armand ate with them. In the afternoon Armand took a nap in the little guest room, which could be locked from the inside, though he found no reason to do that. In the evening the young couple who had visited the day before returned, so Armand emerged from his room and joined them. Soon the twin sister also showed up. She went straight over to Armand, who got up, and they stood facing each other like that; she leaned close and offered him her lips, and he kissed her, long and lingering, surrounded by the homeowners and their friends. Despite the fact that he had come to this little coastal town without expectations, what happened came as quite a surprise to him, because even though he'd known her for a year by this time, they had never behaved like this with each other before.

The twin sister didn't stay long. She pulled Armand into the little guest room and said that he had to be patient. The trip that her parents had planned had been postponed because her father had been involved in some important business matter. But they would be leaving soon, on their long-awaited Easter holiday to far-off Italy. Traveling by air from Bergen. She said nothing about whether N would be going with them, but he knew that she was. N herself had told him as much, even saying that her twin sister would be coming too. So Armand assumed that N was already at her parents' house in this little coastal town, but the twin sister didn't mention her by name. But because of this, Armand didn't leave the house at all until the twin sister finally came to get him four days later.

By this time it was Maundy Thursday, and her parents (along with N) had left for Bergen that same morning to catch the plane to Italy. As they walked along the cul-de-sac, and then entered one of the town's main streets, he was blinded by the bright springtime sun; he felt the wind stinging his face and tearing at his clothes as he allowed himself to be led by the twin sister to her house, which she now had all to herself. It was located in the middle of town, a large, two-story single-family house. It stood in a large yard, which seemed rather bare at this time of year, but it wasn't hard to imagine the yard in full bloom in the summertime when it would undoubtedly be luxuriant. From N he'd heard that her (and her twin sister's) father was one of the most powerful and wealthiest men in the little coastal town, so he was not the least surprised when the twin sister opened the gate and began walking up the drive to what could easily be described as a noble manor house, based on a general notion of how a noble manor house in a coastal Vestland town of minor size should look. The so-called impressive front entry, with its slate steps, solid oak door, and a small porch framed by heavy columns, was no less than what you'd expect to find at the entrance to a noble manor house in a windblown town in Vestland.

But inside! Magnificent rooms filled with gold, silver, and paintings. Carpets on the floor and some on the walls. Wainscoting. Heavy furniture that must have been shipped on vessels that could hardly have had room for any other cargo than these massive pieces. The dining room. Smoking salon. Billiard room. Conservatory. Library. Music room. A single elegant ballroom, with rococo chairs lining the walls. Objets d'art. Antiquities. Venetian glass. Bohemian crystal chandeliers in every room, sometimes several. Heavy drapery. Damask tablecloths. Exquisite flower arrangements. Tapestries. A wine cellar.

The young Armand V. was overwhelmed. Inconceivable

wealth was proclaimed by these rooms. The twin sisters' father must be filthy rich! And all this was only on the first floor. On the second floor were the family's private bedrooms. Armand hardly dared believe his own eyes, not least because he couldn't comprehend how this villa, which didn't look particularly huge from the outside, could contain so many magnificent rooms, and be so capacious; it must be physically impossible, but after the twin sister had led him from one room to another, he had to admit that this was truly what he was now seeing with his own eyes.

But that was later. At first Armand got only a brief glimpse of all these riches because the twin sister led him up to the second floor to her own rooms, the ones she'd had when she was a little girl, which were just the way she'd left them when she went to Oslo to study, and this was where she stayed whenever she came home for brief vacations. There was a sitting room—big, light, and airy—with a door leading to a balcony, and another door standing ajar that led into her bedroom, which was the same size as, no, bigger, than a normal-sized bedroom. For the time being Armand did not go through the half-open door. In the sitting room, the twin sister sat down in an easy chair that was part of a grand sofa group, inviting Armand to take a seat in a matching chair. She gave him a quizzical look and a flirtatious smile. Armand saw that he would have to take the initiative. He stood up and went over to her.

Then he picked her up and carried her through the half-open door and into her bedroom, laying her down on the bed and sating his desire. Only afterward was he able to look around the room. On his knees he straightened up, looming over the languorous, naked twin sister stretched out on the bed with her eyes closed as he observed the setting for the lovemaking that had just occurred. A big room with feminine wallpaper and curtains, with a half-open door to the twin sister's private sitting room. A large dressing table with a huge mirror dominated the room, and two cozy easy chairs with a side table between them stood along one wall. There was also a bookcase and a music table over there, and against the opposite wall was the twin sister's bed, on which Armand was kneeling for the first time. It was rather narrow and seemed somewhat lost in that huge bedroom. If it had been a double bed, or at least a *grand lit*, then it would have taken its natural place in the center of the room, but now it was the bed of a lost young girl that stood there against the wall. A lone young girl's bed amidst all this luxury. Not without charm, but perhaps more a symbol of expected chastity. Along the same wall as the bed was a closed door, and Armand wondered where it led. He would soon find out, because now the twin sister opened her eyes and got out of bed, walking over to open the door, and he saw her go into a bathroom before she shut the door. When she came back out she lay down on the bed again, and Armand crept down next to her. A little later Armand got up and opened the same door and went into the bathroom. Naturally it was very elegant and neat, but what aroused his interest most was that in addition to the door that opened onto the twin sister's bedroom, there was another door, exactly the same, located on the opposite wall. He tried the handle to see if it was locked, but it wasn't, so he pressed down on the handle slowly and cautiously opened the door. He was looking into an almost identical bedroom to the twin sister's, though decorated in different colors, but this room also had a half-open door to a spacious sitting room, and Armand realized that he had opened the bathroom door into N's chambers, so he quickly closed it again. Now he was in a bathroom with two closed doors on opposite walls. There was no third door opening onto a hallway. Armand realized that the two sisters shared a bathroom, which could only be accessed by passing first through one of the sisters' private rooms. He opened the door and was back in the twin sister's large bedroom with her narrow, young girl's bed. They lay there for a long time, both overwhelmed by what had happened, after wishing for it for several weeks.

It was not until afterward that the twin sister gave Armand a tour of the house, one room after the other. It was Maundy Thursday. It was two weeks since the twin sister had suggested that Armand come to visit her over Easter because she would be alone in the big house in the little coastal town in Vestland, and he had taken the train and ferry, traveling for almost twenty-four hours to reach her. For four days he had waited for her in lodgings she'd recommended, and now he'd finally reached the sisters' house and was alone with the twin sister in the home where she'd grown up. Here he stayed for the rest of Easter vacation. On the day after Easter he went back to Oslo, while the twin sister remained to wait for her family's return from their postponed vacation in Italy so she could spend a few days with them. Then she and N would return to their studies in Oslo.

Now Armand was with the twin sister. Armand's attention had previously been drawn to N before her twin sister appeared and issued her surprising invitation. He'd had a close, budding, and even consummated relationship with N. That's why it was so surprising that he found himself in her childhood home in that remote Vestland town together with her twin sister, without N knowing; nor would she ever find out. The days he'd spent with the twin sister had been unforgettable. The twin sister appeared to him in all her sweetness. She loved to display her charms, preferably with a large mirror behind her. N, as the person he thought he knew, was more discreet and reserved when it came to displaying her beauty, the beauty that was hers from birth. Over this Easter holiday Armand had experienced a fairy tale. The twin sister appeared like a princess to Armand in this elegant Vestland house, in her private chambers. His desire was immeasurable, doubtless stimulated by all the surrounding riches, as they slept together in her narrow, young girl's bed. He was quite giddy when he left the little town looking out over the Atlantic on the day after Easter in order to start back on the long journey to Oslo and his studies.

A week later N and her twin sister also showed up in the city. The usual groupings resumed at the table where Armand, the twin sisters, and their friends usually sat. What had seemed, before Easter, to be the introductory phase of a love affair between N and Armand developed into precisely that. Armand entered into a relationship with N. Was that because her twin sister had seemed so aloof toward him when she returned to Oslo after Easter? Not once did she refer to the wonderful time they'd had over the Easter vacation. She never visited him alone again. But did Armand ever venture to visit her? Did he try, desperately, when several of them were sitting at the table, to cryptically allude to what they'd shared in all secrecy over Easter in the little coastal town in Vestland? No, never. If Armand had become nothing more than thin air for her, she had become the same for him. Armand began a relationship with N. That's what had to happen. The fact that Armand had begun an affair with N, the twin sister's twin sister, did not seem to have any effect on her. Strangely enough Armand accepted this; more than that, he found it perfectly natural, and he hardly even considered it at the time. But quite early in his relationship with N, Armand would catch himself searching for what was different in N's voice, what did not exist there, that tiny something that wasn't there, but that had been in her twin sister's voice. The two sisters were almost identical, after all. People who hardly knew them could see no difference, but those who knew them well could see that there was a difference and could tell them apart, without being able to explain or point out what the difference might be; but those who were very close to them, as Armand now was, could say exactly what made N who she was and her twin sister who she was; on the other hand sometimes even Armand mixed them up, as when one of them was standing in a doorway and Armand saw her in silhouette from behind, and for an instant he thought it was N, but then she made a certain movement and he realized it was her twin sister. So it wasn't merely the differences that had developed in their vocal cords that distinguished the two sisters from each other, but other things as well, even though Armand had a clear idea that the other differences had developed based on the difference in their voices. And based on the sweet, faintly different timbre of the two sisters' vocal cords, the swell of their breasts appeared as a clear difference, their breathing was different, the way they inhaled, their way of expressing satisfaction or concealed pain as they exhaled, not least of which because their excitement, their passions, and their disappointments were at such different levels. Sometimes, when Armand was lying with N, he would suddenly wish he was lying with her twin sister. But also the opposite, when he lay with N he was glad that it was N he lay with and not her twin sister, because just then he remembered her twin sister, and recalled that her twin sister had never been the way N was now. Had this become Armand's curse? Was he condemned to compare the two sisters, who were born on the same day, at the same hour? In any event he visited the twin sister again. It could well be that it was after an experience with N that was not of the type first mentioned—meaning that he longed for the twin sister while he lay with N—but of the latter type, meaning he had lain with N and been clearly aware that he, at that moment, was glad to be lying with N, and not with the twin sister, and yet he decided to visit her twin sister again. He visited the twin sister, but was rejected. This repeated itself time after time over the years—not that he was rejected, but that he visited her.

———

9. Was Armand occupied with living a noble life? Who asks such a question in our day? This young student. He looked forward to living a noble life. Yes! Armand looked forward to living a noble life. Serving his country? Serving God? Serving society? Is there anyone who thinks like that anymore? No, fortunately. But I allowed Armand to have that thought, and more than that: without that kind of a thought Armand does not exist.

10. It's only logical that Armand's wedding should also be celebrated here in the footnotes. A modest wedding. In the unwritten novel I would have called it a typical student wedding, with the happy couple and the bridesmaid and best man gathered at Oslo City Hall. With an explanation for why it wasn't held in all splendor at a mansion in a little coastal town in Vestland, but rather as a modern student wedding. After the ceremony the newlyweds and their witnesses dined at a nice restaurant. As most people will have guessed, Armand's bride with the initial N appears in the unwritten novel over there. Way over there. The witnesses were two people who haven't been named so far, and probably won't be mentioned again, a friend of Armand's and a friend of N's. Not Paul Buer, who by this time had disappeared from Armand's life. And not N's twin sister.

11. Decisive years. For Armand's generation the years between twenty-five and thirty were undoubtedly decisive. It had nothing to do with the political circumstances under which they lived, but with how this generation's life path was fundamentally constituted. It was during these years that the big transformation occurred. Childhood and youth receded for good, in favor of an unknown future. People stopped defining themselves in relation to what they used to be in their childhood and youth, and defined themselves exclusively in terms of future opportunities evident in their present situation. They made new friends, and if the friendships lasted it was because they all continued on the same path, and the friendship was sealed

precisely because they both knew, or in any event sensed, that they would be naturally connected later in life as well, even if later they weren't necessarily living in the same place. It was now two years since Armand and Paul had sat in the Krølle over beers after seeing a Godard movie at the Gimle. Since then they hadn't seen each other except for a few brief encounters at the university, in the cafeteria line at Frederikke, or coming out of the university bookstore. They had simply slipped away from each other. They had largely slipped away from each other by the time they met that evening and ended up at the Krølle. It didn't cause any sorrow, any sense of loss. Not until many years later did Armand find himself missing Paul Buer, and by that time it was too late and didn't matter much anyway. Each of them had gotten involved in new relationships, and the youth they had shared growing up in the same city now seemed so remote that it had to be viewed as lost. That's why Armand married N at Oslo City Hall in utter solitude, compared to what he'd imagined when he arrived in Oslo six years earlier. The thought that Paul Buer should have been his best man never even crossed his mind.

––––––––

12. Armand's love life. He married N, but he kept visiting her twin sister time after time over the years. This is a fact that must be explained. It doesn't mean that Armand was unfaithful to N, but that he needed her twin sister in order to love N. Armand experienced his wedding as a bold act. After N and he had decided to get married, he was simply looking ahead: toward happiness. Happiness with N.

13. Double love. The woman up above, whom he was married to, and the woman in the footnotes. Armand's feeling of being locked in a curse persisted until he met the woman who would become his second wife, the mother of his son. The two sisters were almost identical, but operated in two different contexts. As mentioned, he visited the second in order to take possession of the first. Over and over, in his thoughts. N exhibited a high degree of self-control, she did not suffer from false modesty, and her dresses suited her as she moved through her own youthful years. Brightly lit rooms were her specialty. N carried a lamp, her twin sister a flashlight. The twin sister most often wore a gray coat with the collar turned up whenever she went out walking. In the dark she took the flashlight out of her coat pocket to shine on her path as she walked, cautiously but precisely, on the path she never took with Armand, though that was what he longed for. Otherwise they were the same. In the end it turned out that the opposite was also true, that it was the twin sister who carried a lamp, and N who lit the way with a flashlight. But it was the first image that Armand retained, that's just how it was.

14. Maybe he thought the curse would be lifted when he got married, and when offspring came into the marriage. But that didn't happen. The twin sister was not N's bridesmaid because it wouldn't have looked right when the marriage was formalized at Oslo City Hall, if the photo showed the bridegroom with the two identical women at his side, the bride and her bridesmaid, her sister. Otherwise the twin sister visited them often when they lived in

the married-student housing in Sogn. To Armand it seemed to be a dangerous triangle, and he usually found an excuse to avoid it.

---

15. Decisive years. Suddenly he found himself in a town in southeast Norway, working as a teacher at a district community college. With him was N, who was now his wife. She was also a teacher, but at the local secondary school. They had just moved from Oslo, where both had received their degrees from the university. And now they were starting a new life. They lived in a row house, they made new friends, and they were well liked. But Armand hadn't been able to settle in. He pictured himself having a research career at the university, so he was waiting to receive a response to his applications. N got pregnant and gave birth to a daughter. But Armand was still restless. He dreamed of moving on, becoming a researcher. And N didn't want him to settle for the teaching job he had taken. She had big dreams for him. It was the mid-1970s. Then one day a guest lecturer came to town. He knew Armand from before, from when Armand was a student at the university in Blindern. When they met once again, he suggested that Armand should get away from this town in southeast Norway and his job at the community college. He had an idea.

---

16. Armand and the cigarette. A joy to his soul. The fact that I had Armand light a cigarette gives him a special quality, and it would be artistically irresponsible not to make this plain. In the social stratum where Armand now naturally belongs, few people are smokers. I'll refrain from any sarcasm about this

and make do with pointing out that Armand is different. And he makes no effort to hide this difference; on the contrary. A monogrammed cigarette case made of silver is part of his persona. He places it on the table, and when he so desires, he opens the case with a delighted expression and takes out a slender cigarette, which he lights with the greatest pleasure, using a fancy custom lighter. He holds in his hand the slender cigarette, a little wand that he uses when gesturing.

In all his elegance, Armand represents a counterweight. The vulgar Smoking Law, which really should have been called the anti-cigarette law, makes it necessary for an author of my type to choose literary protagonists who are capable of setting the tone in my novels. Even if the novel, as in this instance, is unreadable, or unwritable, and thus has to appear only as footnotes to the novel that should or could have been written, it's important that at least an inkling of a protagonist who is capable of setting the tone breaks through. Such as Armand. The Norwegian ambassador Armand V. A man described as master of the situation. He can decide for himself when he wants a cigarette or doesn't want one for some plausible or tactful reason. A man who tactfully gives smokers occasion to cultivate their minor vices whenever he is the host, and who expects others to behave equally tactfully toward him when he is the guest.

I could go on like this forever. But the main point is that the vulgar Smoking Law will lead to an increased focus on the literary significance of cigarettes. I have to consider how little the characters in my novels have been depicted in relation to the cigarette they're smoking; it has been such a natural thing, both for them and for me, that it hardly needed to be mentioned. But that's over now. It's time to revive the cigarette as a stylish accessory. A literary symbol, something of significance. A prop that unites my century, the twentieth century. Not only does the cigarette unite that century, it also asserts a connection, a narrow elegant line, reaching into the new century, like a historical demonstration. Pointing back to the cigarette-smoking movie stars, which personified male elegance on the big screen, and to those mysterious women, those divas, with their cigarette holders. A lifestyle that's about to disappear, and soon only the novel can save it from extinction.

Hence this portrait of Armand. Full-length. Posed. As he smokes a cigarette. The hysteria of the age has not set its mark on his facial features, protected as he is by the mysterious bluish smoke that surrounds his partially erased body and rises up into the air, toward the ceiling in the room as he holds the cigarette like a little weapon. When Armand plays host at the Norwegian Embassy, in a prominent city somewhere abroad, he discreetly ensures that those who can't stand the sight of a cigarette, or the smoke that rises from a lit cigarette won't have to suffer. He makes sure that a small room is made available to the smokers, a small sitting area or even his own elegant office. In this way he separates those hypochondriacs from those who are mortal. And he makes a point of spending time with each group. But that's no reason to hide, at least not in these lines, that he prefers to join the mortals, since he too is just that.

_____

17. It was no coincidence that Armand was in the diplomatic corps, although the instigating event was actually a coincidence.

He could just as well have taken a job at the university or perhaps in publishing, but he became a diplomat, because once he grew accustomed to thinking of himself as a future diplomat, he couldn't imagine being anything else. At that point he didn't know why he'd never thought of it before, and he regarded the two years that had passed since he finished his university degree as wasted (he'd spent that time as a teacher at a district community college). He couldn't understand it, especially because his educational background seemed custom-made for a future career with the Norwegian foreign service. He had a minor in both German and French, which meant that he spoke three foreign languages fluently (for those slow on the uptake: German, French, and English), and his major was history. Instead of writing his thesis on a topic within Norwegian history, which was the most common for university students, he had chosen instead European history, specifically the geographic areas on both sides of the Rhine river, titling his thesis "Border Conflicts Between France and the German-Speaking States from the Seventeenth Century to 1950, or from the Thirty Years' War to the Establishment of the European Coal and Steel Community (ECSC)." This sounds like a treatise that could have been commissioned by the Norwegian Government anno 1972, yet it might also be suitable as an application for entry into that same government's foreign service. But the truth was that this thesis was written by someone who opposed the European Economic Community (EEC); he was in fact a staunch EEC opponent who at that time had no dreams of entering the Norwegian foreign service, nor did he wish to become an editor for a publishing company. But when the opportunity arose a couple of years later and he had time to consider the matter, he jumped at the chance.

He wouldn't deny—especially to himself, either then or now—that he'd found a real temptation in the comfort and glamour enveloping the diplomatic life. When you find yourself in a situation where you, in all seriousness, can picture yourself as a future diplomat, then the thought of all the conspicuous glory, which would subsequently follow and literally surround you, was irresistible. For this young man, who was twenty-eight at the time, the mere thought of serving in the most fascinating capitals in some of the world's most popular countries and living not in third-class hotels with only cold-water taps and narrow, nasty, creaking beds, but in small, elegant apartments in the middle of Europe's hub (as he put it)—which he assumed the Norwegian foreign service would, of course, make available, even for the lowliest of secretaries in the embassy in Paris, and for the most part this turned out to be true—all of this was enough to make him dizzy. It wasn't even the thought of cities such as Paris, Rome, Buenos Aires, and Mexico City, or countries such as France, Italy, Argentina, and Mexico that stirred a yearning in him; it was the thought that the whole world stood open to him, from Mongolia to Honduras, and he felt enticed by the very idea of being assigned a posting, regardless of where, and the fact that he wouldn't know in advance where he'd be going; that seemed to him like a truly attractive lottery, which spoke to his heart and soul. In short: Armand V. seized the opportunity. He applied for admittance to the course given by the Ministry of Foreign Affairs for aspiring candidates, and was, we almost say "of course," accepted.

Can a young, serious-minded person like Armand V. allow his career choice to be guided by something so banal as the thought of the comfortable life awaiting him if only he grabs a pen and fills out an application for the foreign ministry's own course for future diplomats? Yes, that's possible, but it wasn't the only factor. When Armand first began thinking about the possibility of becoming a diplomat, he was also attracted by the actual work carried out by a diplomat, and especially what his own role might entail. Armand had certain personal tendencies that drew him to the Norwegian foreign service, tendencies that were quite evident to his friends and acquaintances. The previously mentioned thesis in history was one expression of these tendencies. Considering the topic, it was as if the subject had been handpicked by a young, dreary EEC supporter, while Armand was actually an opponent of the EEC, and that was why he'd chosen such a dry, pro-EEC topic; he'd even presented the prime argument for why the EEC was such a huge success for Europe's suffering people, and he did so with ferocious joy. It wasn't that he had arrived at a conclusion that depicted a clear anti-EEC point of view; no, he treated his subject almost like a dull and—you have to admit in this instance—ardent EEC supporter would have done, though less dryly and, let's not forget, far less zealously. At the center of the irreconcilable forces in the EEC battle was Armand V., calmly recounting the history of the French-German border conflicts over the course of three hundred and fifty years, and this was of utterly no use to any EEC opponents. At least presumably it wasn't. But if you took his thesis seriously and read what he'd written, it turned out that this dry and ardent EEC supporter, Armand's fictional antipode, couldn't use the thesis for anything. And that was their central argument! What do you know? What do you know? No doubt Armand's friends saw this, because when Armand told them that he'd applied and been accepted into the course offered by the Royal Norwegian Ministry of Foreign Affairs for candidates to the foreign service, they initially stared at him and exclaimed: You???!!!, but then added: Sure, why not?

When Armand now—here in this footnote and not in the novel up above—looks back on his life working for the Norwegian foreign ministry, as I, the author, have understood it, he will undoubtedly conclude that deep in his heart it was probably the thought of the game itself that made him a diplomat. But what sort of game? That remained unclear. What was clear, however, was that he was a radical young man who was tempted and subsequently allowed himself to be enticed in an attempt to achieve a way of life, or a professional career, by seeking admittance to the Norwegian foreign service, which, for its part, was connected to the world's mightiest superpower, the United States, with such established ties that even someone with leftist leanings had to realize it was sheer protest politics to support the idea that Norway should conduct an independent foreign policy, even if this were desirable, and an individual found it important to display this desire by stepping forward as a protester and declaring himself an opponent of NATO, as Armand did. But what game was it that Armand envisioned within these established structures when he imagined himself a newly hired employee in the Norwegian foreign service, for instance as a fourth secretary in the embassy in Brussels? It's difficult to know. Presumably Armand V. must have been intrigued by the paradoxical nature of the situation in which he would turn into a Norwegian foreign service officer, and that may have caused him to regard it as a game, which it certainly was not, as he would soon find out. He had landed in a paradox. The young diplomat was a paradox in his own eyes. That's probably how we might view it.

But as a young diplomat, the paradoxical nature of Armand V. as an individual was of concern only to himself. The work assigned to a young man in the foreign service, either at home in Norway or abroad, is not the sort that invites thoughts about whether it's a game, as Armand preferred to call it, or a paradox. It's routine work, pure and simple, that is carried out for years. Although it can be routine work that seems supremely attractive to anyone who has a weakness for glamour, it's still routine work. Routine work in the higher echelons, as Armand V., the experienced diplomat, might have characterized it. Armand did a good job of mastering this routine work and rose through the ranks and was entrusted with so-called bigger assignments (in reality they weren't so big!), until, after fourteen years, he became an ambassador at the age of forty-two, which could be described as a meteoric career.

In other words, the young radical had done well. The paradox had enjoyed a meteoric career. And what's interesting about this is: he'd done it without in any way changing his fundamental attitude toward the political game or the role of his own country in said game. The forty-two-year-old, newly appointed Norwegian ambassador to Jordan had precisely the same attitude toward the United States as when he'd applied to the foreign service, and the now aging diplomat continues to maintain these same attitudes, carrying them, strictly speaking, inside his own heart, even though the game is no longer the same. And that's actually not so strange. An ordinary, enlightened person of Armand's generation was, of course, against the Vietnam War and quite immune personally to American rhetoric. Immune to and skeptical about American politics in general, and often deeply scornful, though this was not something he could express.

Yet he had no major problems with working for a foreign service that was to such a large extent within the sphere of American influence. He entered the diplomatic corps during the Cold War, was appointed to his first ambassador position during the Cold War, and even though he was originally a strong opponent of NATO, the arguments in favor of Norway's membership in NATO were so irrefutable that he could easily not so much promote them, since that wasn't necessary, but at least use them as a basis for his actions, no matter in which echelon he found himself. The Cold War was a reality, and Norway's place as a friend of the U.S., guaranteed by the United States (and NATO), was an irrefutable reality. This was called Norway's national security policy, and it was irrefutable. The Cold War was a reality, and if you said that Norway had made a definitive choice, that's not true. Norway had not made a choice, there was no choice to be made, and thus Norway's choice was not definitive. Armand could not entertain any other thoughts on this subject. It was a fact.

But when the Cold War was over, a different situation naturally ensued. Not for him personally—since his only subsequent problem was that he had to make sure he celebrated the victory in an appropriately diplomatic manner—but for the whole world, which now was of course turned upside down, though with the United States remaining Norway's friend and guarantor as well as the world's one and only superpower. Many harbored a hope that Europe would be allowed to play a more independent role, and with regard to the United States, a more challenging role. Armand V., who liked to call himself a European—which is also an apt description, considering his literary, cinematic, artistic, and linguistic references—was, however, not greatly optimistic, at least not in terms of his own foreign service. He regarded this sort of new evaluation as political wishful thinking, which the political decision-makers in his small country apparently wanted to label as security-oriented adventurist policy, and when people now talked about the possibility that Norway might join the EU in order to have an impact, it was probably so that the country could become allied with the former Eastern Bloc, including Poland, Lithuania, Latvia, Estonia, the Czech Republic, Slovakia, and Hungary, trying to hold back the eventual objectives of the traditional major powers in Europe, such as Germany and France, to establish a common European foreign policy independent of the United States. Norway's strong bond with the U.S. would most certainly, in a tense political situation between the EU and Norway, cause Norway to become a welcome agent working on behalf of the interests of the United States, and Armand V. was not looking forward to this potential situation, though he would of course loyally abide by it when carrying out his diplomatic duties. It should be unnecessary even to mention the latter part of the previous sentence; in fact, it should have been left out, since it was sufficient to say that he did not look forward to the eventuality of such a situation, which is something a European like himself should be allowed to admit, at least to himself and also to others, if anyone, contrary to expectation, should happen to ask the aging Ambassador V. for his views and had the professional clout to demand his opinion.

Armand had mastered the game. It gave him a deep sense of satisfaction to do so; it was almost pleasurable. But what was his intention in conducting this so-called game? There was no real reward in it. But for some reason—and you're welcome to call it a paradoxical reason—he felt useful. He could say that he was serving his country, although that was not something he said. On the other hand, he did claim, openly and loudly, that it was his job to promote Norway's interests. These were not merely nice words but an apt description of what his job entailed. The fact that it was not his own interests he served, in one way or another, and maybe not even as the primary focus, but rather what others defined as Norway's interests, was something that he'd managed to live with during the thirty years he'd been attached to the Norwegian foreign service.

He probably wouldn't have joined the foreign service if not for the fact that it also offered him great personal satisfaction. If, initially, he'd been an avowed friend of the United States and everything America stood for, and in addition had been the same person he was now, if such a person was even possible, then he wouldn't have been sufficiently tempted to seek admittance to the foreign service, even if the opportunity had presented itself, and he would have had to give careful thought to whether this was a career path for him. It would have been too highfalutin for him. He would have choked on his own words, even though, of course, he would then have served Norway's interests, now as then.

He wouldn't have been able to say that he served Norway's interests, even though he would have been in compliance, in every way, with his own attitude toward the United States, which in this instance was in agreement with the official attitude.

No, he would have swallowed those words, finding them repellent. The only thing he could have said was that he was glad to be living in a small country which had positioned itself so wisely that he, as a Norwegian diplomat, could serve America's interests. The fact that he, in that case—and explicitly assuming that he was precisely the same person as he was now—could have expressed himself in such a manner was because he would have been saddled with a low sense of national identity.

That would have been no problem for him. He would have liked to emphasize, even to other people if an opportunity presented itself, that he had a low sense of national identity. In the instance we're now picturing (meaning that from a young age, Armand was an ardent fan of the United States and everything that country represented), it was because of his low sense of national identity that he could express the truth about himself as a diplomat: meaning he was happy to be part of a foreign service that had positioned itself so wisely that he, as a Norwegian diplomat, could serve America's interests. Grand words, but true. Could he, considering the *actual* reality in which he found himself, say something comparable?

It would have to be something like this: He was happy to belong to a foreign service that had managed to establish such strong ties between our small country and the most powerful nation in the world, because this was undeniably, considering the state of reality, in the interests of our own small country. Could he say that? Well, wasn't that what he did say, time and again, even in these footnotes? Yes. He could indeed say this, based on his point of view, and with his low sense of national identity.

But here we might counter with another question: What could Armand have said if he'd had a high sense of national identity? If he'd had this high sense of national identity but otherwise was the exact same person he was. It turns out this Armand would be unthinkable. We cannot imagine Armand with a high sense of national identity, that's impossible, he wouldn't exist if equipped with that. We might imagine him, albeit reluctantly, as an ardent supporter of the United States, but not at the same time in possession of a high sense of national identity. We might think of others, of course, as real people equipped in such a way; in fact, we can imagine hundreds of thousands of Norwegians who love America and who are at the same time possessed of a high sense of national identity; there are undoubtedly hundreds of such people within the Norwegian foreign service itself, but Armand is not one of them, that's simply unthinkable.

These labyrinthine perceptions, these distinctions between the fictional and factual Armand-personality, the thinkable and the unthinkable, between paradox and social status, between who Armand is and who it might be possible for him to be, all of which I have here presented in examples, formed the basis for Armand's intellectual maneuverings in terms of his outward and social daily life, in that he appeared to be a highly affable diplomat when associating with diplomats from other countries, or with Norwegians, whose interests he did his utmost to promote, whether it be economic, humanitarian, political, or cultural. Yes, Armand had a low sense of national identity, but he couldn't be imagined any other way. He was a man with a low sense of national identity, but such men do exist. And it has been part of him for the thirty years he has worked for the foreign service, and even longer. Yet, in spite of this, he was able to carry out the rituals that a national identity required of him. And speak Norwegian. He spoke three other languages fluently, and the joy of being able to speak fluent English, German, and French was grounded in his Norwegian identity. He didn't say that he spoke fluent Norwegian, no, he was Norwegian; and because of his Norwegianness, he'd learned English, German, and French so that he could speak these languages fluently. Of course a Czech would say the same thing, but so what? Wouldn't a Czech also enjoy speaking fluent English, and in the same way, because of the incomprehensibility of his Czechishness, just as Armand spoke fluent English because of the incomprehensibility of his Norwegianness? Have a look! There, in that majestic hall, among lofty company, wearing white tie and tails, those two are speaking fluent English together, the Norwegian and the Czech diplomats, at a ball in Vienna. Armand's Norwegianness expressing itself in fluent English. This was his national identity, and he never forgot it for a moment.

For all of his adult life Armand had held a position that required him to relate in a positive way to the Norwegian national symbols and what we call Norwegian values. He spent his workdays in rooms where the Norwegian flag had a prominent place and where big photographs of King Olav V hung on the wall, and since 1991, of King Harald V and Queen Sonja. These official rooms, for the most part, were situated in luxurious villas, which also housed his private residence, since it's customary to divide an embassy into official and private sections. Most recently it was the embassy in Budapest, where Armand was the Norwegian envoy until he was summoned back to the foreign ministry in Oslo a couple of years ago. Surrounded by Norwegian flags, and with big photographs of the royal couple in a prominent place on the wall in the official reception hall, he acted in Budapest as Norway's representative. With no sense of irony whatsoever. He welcomed his guests, as he stood next to the big Norwegian flag. For example, on May 17, Norwegian Constitution Day. The guests included invited Norwegians, who were either permanent or temporary residents in Hungary, as well as Hungarian associates—friends of Norway you might call them—and members of the diplomatic corps. The Norwegian ambassador, in his own eyes the game player, or the paradox, raised his glass and offered a toast to His Majesty the King and Her Majesty the Queen, speaking in a dignified and natural manner.

Armand was impressive. As he should be after so many years in the foreign service. But even as a young embassy secretary he had known how to carry out his minor assignments with dignity. He seemed natural, even sincere. And in a sense, that's precisely what I am, thought Armand. But it's not hard to appear natural and sincere when you have such a pleasant job as I have, he added, speaking to himself. The position of ambassador must be one of the most ideal jobs for anyone in his sixties. Everything is arranged for you. Living quarters. A chauffeur-driven car. Travel reservations. Courier mail. A staff of intelligent people who understand your smallest wish. The surroundings are comfortable, even elegant, sometimes outright luxurious. There are frequent meetings with interesting people. Frequent invitations. Receptions, lunches, dinners. He himself hosted receptions, lunches, and dinners. He could bring in a chef for a specific occasion, or hire one on a permanent basis. The latter depended on what was most beneficial in terms of the number of diners and the costs involved in whatever country he happened to be stationed, which in this case was Hungary. Armand had no complaints. He knew that he was highly privileged; nor did he have any problem with setting a price on these privileges of his. He sometimes counted himself lucky to be an ambassador for a small country instead of a big country with serious ambitions, which he thought would have presented much more trouble. More things to worry about, both in terms of protocol and other matters. The pressure would have been far greater.

There was a strict and formal set of rules to which he had to adhere. But this wasn't difficult, because it came naturally to an experienced ambassador. He knew which invitations he *had* to accept and which ones he *could* accept; he knew to which events he could send the embassy counselor or first secretary, and which invitations he ought to politely decline. The same held for the invitations he himself sent out. What separated a good ambassador from a not-so-good ambassador, so to speak, was the degree to which an ambassador was able to behave informally within the formal framework, and thereby establish informal contacts that might prove useful for the small country he served. These informal contacts might be people who were able to provide useful information about what was really going on in the country, situations about which the official, public sources failed to give enough information; it could also mean people who had good financial connections, which he could then pass on to Norwegian businesspeople who were interested in dealing with or within the country, and Hungary fell into the latter case. It's no exaggeration to say that Armand was a master at establishing these sorts of contacts. For this reason he could allow himself to adopt a rather bold manner with regard to the Norwegian foreign ministry. He did this because he assumed it enhanced his reputation within the ministry. He assumed that his bold way of behaving helped to divert attention from what might have been perceived as more suspect qualities that he possessed, whatever they might be.

He liked looking at himself and his environs from the outside. Both openly, during an event, when all the celebrities were present, as he said, but also when he was alone. He couldn't even count how many nights he would retreat to his private quarters, drop his diplomatic attire in a heap on the bedroom floor, and then climb into bed, pulling the covers up to his ears and retracing everything that had happened over the course of the evening as he chuckled somewhat maliciously, sometimes laughing till he gasped, until the next day dawned, and he fell asleep, exhausted from laughing at someone else's expense. This was his great strength, and he knew it. The ministry knew it too, though in a different way. Even though he kept these night-time laughing sessions secret from everyone, his colleagues in the top echelons of the foreign ministry knew that Armand V. harbored thoughts and ideas behind his mask that were not the same as the ones he so loyally expressed; they may have even suspected that he in some way or other laughed himself silly when he was in his own bed, thinking about his life and career.

Had he ever had a secret desire to upset the game? Had he dreamt of the moment when he could cast aside the mask and show his true face? No. If he'd had such a wish, he wouldn't have dared make a career within the foreign service. He wore a mask, but he'd never felt an urge to cast it aside, in one dreadful moment, so as to show his true face. Could this be called Armand's unswerving loyalty? It's possible, thought Armand, yes, that's entirely possible. That's why they trust me.

As an example of Armand's style within the Norwegian foreign service, it might be mentioned that he could easily say to the foreign minister, if at the time the minister happened to be a social democrat: It's clear that the Cold War was expensive; it was a war, after all. But we can no longer afford to continue paying these costs. There's no reason to continue paying war costs in a time of peace. I'm thinking about all these welfare benefits, pensions, health-care benefits, unemployment benefits, lengthy vacations, and sky-high salaries. They have to be cut back because they're superfluous. Previously they were necessary, they were what we used to fight the enemy. And they were effective. The enemy had to wall up all of East Berlin so that people wouldn't come fleeing to us. But now people will have to make do with Freedom.

And what did the social democratic foreign minister reply to this? That's not known, but he probably considered his answer carefully, because he knew that the unswervingly loyal Ambassador V. wore a mask, and that in private he might not mean a word of what he was now saying in his official capacity.

The foreign minister was younger than Armand. Armand had spent more than thirty years in the foreign service, and in that sense he was a veteran. He carried his age well. He had now been back in Norway for a year; he was at the disposition of the ministry, as it stated in the King's report in Council when his appointment ended as ambassador in Budapest. This meant an advisory capacity and shorter special assignments. In the meantime, he was waiting for the ambassador posting in Paris, or if need be in Brussels, to become available. That would be his crowning achievement, and at the same time, most likely represent his last assignment as Norway's envoy to a foreign nation. Occasionally it occurred to him how astonishing it was that he'd done so well, all things considered. Yet it seemed to him equally astonishing that he'd never really expected this to happen thirty years ago; back then he'd suspected that at some time in the future, he would end up in such a situation that it would prove impossible for him to continue. But they trust me, he thought, they really do. And it's because they know that I live in a linguistic prison which I can't possibly escape.

Did Armand live in a linguistic prison? The answer, of course, is: yes, though it has to be added: it was of his own choosing. Armand would have agreed with such a statement. For him, it had been worth the price. Besides, what was so extraordinary about the fact that Armand had spent thirty years in a linguistic prison? It would have to be that his linguistic prison was a gilded cage, and thus quite conspicuous. But didn't most people within our victorious culture, who were of Armand's caliber and had similar backgrounds to his, live in a linguistic prison?

The difference was that Armand V. knew he lived in a linguistic prison, and he knew he could do nothing else but live in it. The difference was that Armand V. knew this was also something known (about him) by anyone who had ever had control over his career. And it also meant that there were a number of opportunities he hadn't taken. To that he merely shrugged.

He was a knowledgeable man, he was a connoisseur of European literature, film, music, and art from the past to the present day. He had never been stationed anywhere, during all those years, without becoming familiar with the country's literature, film, music, and art; this was equally true of countries outside our cultural circle. He was familiar with the theaters, national art galleries, museums, opera houses, and newspapers in all the capital cities where he'd been stationed. As the ambassador of a small country, he'd had time for all this. What did it mean that in this situation he had found himself for over thirty years in a linguistic prison? It meant that his thoughts were free, but the language was a prison. That he was free when he read his books, but a linguistic prisoner when he carried out the duties of his prominent position.

So you'd think that Armand would have felt moved whenever, on rare occasions, he heard shouts from down on the streets, loud shouts of opinions similar to those he himself felt inclined to express, the measured outbursts of demonstrators, slogans that reverberated through the streets and reached him where he stood behind the bars of language, recognizing this language, which was his, after all, from deep inside him. But no. Armand rejected those who shouted. He rejected the demonstrators. Even when they spoke reflexively in newspaper editorials. They didn't know what they were talking about, he thought then, they don't know anything.

What is it they didn't know? What was it Armand knew? What is it Armand had experienced? The fact that no one can escape power? That no one can escape reality? Most likely. It's hard to imagine he thinks anything else when, on rare occasions, he hears demonstrators shouting his own, innermost words down on the streets, or reads them in newspaper editorials. You might say that his own words are much too far away from him, and that it's those selfsame experiences he has had that distance him from his own words.

This was when Armand was back home in Norway, when he stood at the window of his office on Victoria Terrace and heard shouts from down on the street. Yet even as he rejected these shouts from below, he looked with great confidence to art. He was drawn to art. It was from there that relief would come. It was from there that the words would come. Only art was free. Armand had great faith in the possibilities of art, even though he often felt disappointed at the results produced. He looked almost with envy at the artists. Those who, like him, had their reasons. But unlike him, they were lucky to have possibilities for unfettered expression. They had a rare opportunity, which no one else had. Then why did they so seldom seize that opportunity? They have no idea how lucky they are, thought Armand, they have no idea what an opportunity they have. Because if they did know, they would have seized the chance. I chose my life, long ago, and I know what I've missed out on. Everything, the artists can allow themselves, and yet they only apparently allow themselves; they pretend to do this, yet they almost never actually do it; and since they almost never do it, you can't label it a sin. But if anything can be called a sin, that has to be it, Armand thought sadly. Think what a relief it would be for someone like me, he added. To see it in black and white, he repeated.

───────────

18. In all secrecy, and at any rate without connection to the text above, or far away, Armand had sought out the twin sister, while wearing a gold ring on his finger (Yours, N). This time she received him warmly, telling him that she had no idea what to say. After that, Armand frequently returned, and they would sit and talk about all sorts of things until there finally formed a connection, a reason.

───────────

19. Something told her that there was something wrong. Something told her that she'd been betrayed by the man who said he hadn't betrayed her. Something told her that even if he didn't believe he'd betrayed her, he had in fact betrayed her. Even though she didn't find anything when she went through his pockets, she was still convinced that something lay hidden there, something she should have seen but didn't see, no matter how hard she tried. It's probably much closer than I could ever imagine, she thought. So close that for the life of me I can't see it.

───────────

20. What could she know? Nothing with regard to what Armand feared she might know. She felt insulted, but that couldn't be it. She felt ignored, but isn't everyone ignored by

those who are closest to them? Even when she truly felt she was closest, and didn't merely imagine she was. Had she begun to suspect that she was not, in fact, closest to him? But who then would it be? That was not something she could know, unless someone who was close to Armand revealed the truth, but he couldn't believe that would happen. Yet she felt betrayed, even though she couldn't point to any reason for this feeling. That was enough. She ripped the veil aside, showed her face, and left.

––––––––––

21. Armand meticulously studied her expressions. He understood that she was looking for some sign that he had betrayed her, but he knew she wouldn't find any, unless she planted it there herself. He was afraid she might do that, because she had begun to set traps for him. She tried to put words in his mouth. She often asked him about some meaningless thing and then took note if he diverged in his explanation from what he'd previously said about that same thing. Her irritation grew beyond measure, because she couldn't pin anything on him, and he realized that in the end there was nothing she could do but plant something on him, a handwritten note with an unambiguous message, and that it was only a matter of time before this would happen, and what would he say then? It would be best to confess, he thought. Once and for all. Since there's something standing between us anyway.

––––––––––

22. Armand regarded himself as an enlightened individual. He acknowledged his cynicism, thinking that without it he wouldn't

be able to orient himself in life. He also thought that if it could be said that he, Armand, was not striving to live a noble life, then he didn't deserve to live at all. But he failed to understand that this contradicted the cynicism he enjoyed spreading around, which was what made him so well suited to a diplomatic life. And yet he became a victim of love. He believed in love and despaired at the notion that it might fade. He was young back then, yet well past thirty, and if we picture the despair of this almost thirty-five-year-old embassy secretary at the notion that love might fade, it seems a romantic gesture that's remarkable, although most people will recognize in themselves this inner gesture, because so many share this fixation on the circumstances of erotic love in our time. For Armand, his fear that love might fade meant that he preferred a relationship marked by distrust and a hatred that might violently flare at any moment. The former was inexpressibly sad; the latter was a response to this, and a terrible thing.

---

23. Where did this devotion to love as a phenomenon come from? Is it a remnant of puberty that no one wants to forget, no matter how painful it may be, wanting to remember it instead as a reminder to be ready and prepared for a repetition? One more time! One more time! How much is biology, and how much is cultural learning? Couldn't you settle for eroticism, the fact that two people meet, for just one more time! and then they go their separate ways, back to their own meandering lives which, seen from the perspective of age, in spite of everything, when you look back, is the essence of a person's life, the very symbol, even though it was two people who encountered each other. And

don't seek back to a twin sister's twin sister, who may be the heart of sweetness but not its source. The source is concealed behind layer upon layer of repetition, but for Armand it stopped with the twin sister, something that is revealed as a secret, since the twin sister exists only in these lines.

———————

24. About N and Armand up there. They're married now, of course. They're married through an endless series of book pages; and if these pages had been written down, you could have turned one after the other and read about their marriage until it ended. I see that it has ended now. It happened in Cairo, where Armand was first secretary at the Norwegian embassy. N went back home to Norway, taking along their daughter. That little child has to recover from all this, he has to forget her. As of today, he has not seen N again.

———————

25. It was with a certain uneasiness that Armand now thought back on his marriage to N. This uneasiness is not because of the secret twin sister; rather, it has to do with his falling in love with and marrying N, an experience he chooses to view in isolation. Those were crucial years. Making big decisions that would mark him for life. When he now thought back, he couldn't understand how it had even been possible for him to make those choices, smiling so easily, feeling as carefree as he had. The game of chance. Carefree youth. Carefree male youth. He set out with no thought of consequences and laid siege to her. The young Armand succeeded in affecting the young woman who

would become his wife such that she opened her mind to this idea of the woman toward which Armand's infatuation was directed, and somewhat reluctantly she began to impersonate her in order to find out who she was and what sort of emotions were being directed toward her, until she actually began to believe in them herself. She wanted to be that woman, and she fell in love. She became desired, and blind. She greedily allowed herself to be wrapped in the essence of love and reciprocated. In a state of mutual intoxication they met in a higher sphere and worshipped every movement that each directed toward the other. They were so high up, high up in the spheric realm, that they noticed only the other's image of themselves. But it was Armand who had set this all in motion and who now had to steer and encourage her at these dangerous heights where nothing could satisfy her any longer except for his infatuated image of her, which she had now made her own and which he had to affirm again and again. Thinking about this foreplay before his marriage now made Armand uneasy, now that he was an aging man so many years later. Because the whole thing had been so coincidental, and when it came right down to it, all his flirtations were merely something he had invented. He had been so in love with her, but that was merely something he had invented. Even back then he'd known this was the case. Is this true for everybody? the young Armand had wondered, or am I all alone in this? If that's the case, then who am I?

---

26. After the antagonistic split with N, he was left with the twin sister. The game was over. The twin sister became the wise White Lady. She settled high in the mountains, and Armand

would often visit. He took long walks with the twin sister, who ran a bed-and-breakfast.

————

27. Armand V.'s degree was in history, and occasionally he missed being a practicing historian. Strangely enough, this yearning would come over him particularly when he was sent to one of our stations abroad, because then he wouldn't have much time to devote to his studies of history. Then you might see him, on one of his rare free evenings, sitting in his office with the reading lamp turned on, immersed in big historical tomes. The places might change—it could be Amman, Belgrade, Mexico City, Madrid, Budapest, etc.—but everywhere the scene was the same: our man poring over hefty historical tomes and dreaming that he'd be able to write a historical dissertation on the topic he was studying. But that never happened. This was one of the unfulfilled aspects of Armand's life, and sometimes it nagged at him; but if it had nagged enough, then he might have done something about it, meaning he could have returned to his original field of study and adopted a professional career. He was fully aware of this, so the resignation he felt in terms of this impossible intention was genuine enough. This was felt sometime in 1993 or 1994 when he was busily engaged in making plans for a radical revision of *Aschehoug's History of the World*.

Aschehoug's History of the World was published in the period 1982–86, with the last volume appearing in 1993. Taking into account Armand's theories and plans for revisiting it, we need to present an overview of these sixteen volumes:

Vol. 1: (In the beginning) Up until 1200 BC
Vol. 2: (Advanced civilizations take shape) 1200–200 BC

Armand's interest in revising this *History of the World* made its appearance one day in 1993. That was when the sixteenth and final volume arrived at the residence of the Norwegian ambassador in Madrid. At that time the Norwegian ambassador to Spain was Armand V. He solemnly placed the sixteenth and final volume on the bookshelf in his private quarters. Then he surveyed the entire set as it stood on the shelf, one volume after another, in chronological order. He stepped close to the bookcase, and since this was the day on which the entire *History of the World* was finally complete, in all sixteen volumes, he pulled out one volume after another and perused the number on the spine, the title of each specific volume, and what period of time it covered. Quietly he read the words aloud, with great solemnity but with a furrow on his brow that got deeper and deeper. When he was done, he exclaimed, though still quietly—no, now he said it quite loudly: What the hell? Here we have a *History of the World* which covers my own life in no less than four volumes. And I haven't even turned fifty. Where will it all end!

Then and there Armand decided to put together a plan for an entirely new *History of the World*, to be published under the title: *Aschehoug's Revised History of the World*. Since it was *Aschehoug's History of the World* that he was determined to totally transform, he decided he would stay within the framework of sixteen volumes; this would be an unalterable condition. So he was strictly forbidden to expand the number to twenty or twenty-five volumes, even seventeen volumes would not be permitted, he was strictly forbidden to be tempted to even *think* of an extra volume. Even if he should find an editing mode that was perfectly suited to, for example, a *History of the World* in eighteen volumes, this would be outside the premises that served as the basis for the new *Aschehoug's Revised History of the World*.

Night after night, whenever he had a chance—and that was not often—he would stay up into the wee hours, pondering this project. It was more difficult than he'd imagined, because if he happened to get a good idea, it would soon collide with another idea. Not until March 1994 did the truly brilliant idea occur to him, the final idea, and it glittered in all its mathematical simplicity. He found a mathematical key to dividing up the material. He calculated how many years Aschehoug's current *History of the World* covered. Not wanting to be unreasonable, he started with the year at the beginning of volume 2, which was 1200 BC. If he'd started with the rise of the first nascent cultures, he could have begun as early as approximately 6000 BC, but he found that unreasonable from a mathematical point of view; it was right to start with 1200 BC, the era that saw the first advanced civilizations. This meant that he would cover 3200 years of history (1200 + 2000 = 3200) in sixteen volumes. This meant, in turn, and still from a mathematical point of view, that each volume would contain 3200 years ÷ 16 = *200 years* of history. My time on earth is just as important as yours. Running throughout history is a ceaselessly precious flood of time. Hence: Vol. 1: 1200–1000 BC; Vol. 2: 1000–800 BC; Vol. 3: 800–600 BC; Vol. 4: 600–400 BC; Vol. 5: 400–200 BC; Vol. 6: 200 BC–AD 0; Vol. 7: AD 0–200; Vol. 8: AD 200–400. At this point we're halfway through the development of human history, as best we can understand and survey it. And still to come are both the Western Roman and the Eastern Roman empires, both Rome and Byzantium. Vol. 9: 400–600; Vol. 10: 600–800. As you see, the 10th volume of what is a specifically planned sixteen-volume work ends with the crowning of Charlemagne as the Holy Roman Emperor, in the Franks' own capital of Aachen, but Byzantium is yet to come. Vol. 11: 800–1000. Of course it's possible to choose to begin this volume with the crowning of Charlemagne instead of placing it at the end of volume 10, but Byzantium is yet to come. Vol. 12: 1000–1200. Vol. 13: 1200–1400. Vol. 14: 1400–1600. Only in this volume does Byzantium fall. Vol. 15: 1600–1800. Vol. 16: 1800–2000. (In reality, ending in 1945.)

---

28. But all of this was mere speculation on his part. And these big volumes he was reading? They weren't necessarily intended as part of his plan to put together *Aschehoug's Revised History of*

the World. But they ended up being part of the project, and that was how you might find him, bowed over those hefty, leather-bound books in the glow of his desk lamp. After the idea had occurred to him and he put together the plan, he would often, on the rare free evenings he had, sit there reading *Aschehoug's History of the World*, the whole time editing the volumes in the back of his mind. The closer he got to his own era, the more he valued and venerated his own project. In fact, he felt a sense of triumph on behalf of history itself. On behalf of everyone who had lived before him, especially prior to 1750. Armand studied this contemporary view of history, the whole time keeping his own revised version in the back of his mind. He regarded this process as a way of training his historical sense. Veneration for the concept of time. He had a clear feeling that he was training his lost ability to show historical discipline.

Gradually he grew bolder. He no longer saw any reason to begin with the first advanced civilizations (in approx. 1200 BC), but instead went all the way back to the very first traces of cultures. This meant he could go all the way back to approx. 6000 BC, and then each of the sixteen volumes had to comprise 6000 + 2000 = 8000 ÷ 16 = 500 years. He thought this was an excellent idea, since it reinforced, rather than weakened, the historical consciousness and our understanding of the passage of human history here on earth. He could also have gone further back, to the traces of human civilization in 10,000 BC or so, but he chose 6000 BC, linking it to the first settlement in Çatal Hüyük in what is today Anatolia. Vol. 1: 6000 –5500 BC; Vol. 2: 5500–5000 BC; Vol. 3: 5000–4500 BC; Vol. 4: 4500–4000 BC; Vol. 5: 4000–3500 BC. These first five volumes could be marvelous. They would deal exclusively with traces in the form of actual strata and excavations, as well as in the form of myths. Archaeology and myths. Five of the sixteen volumes about the history of humankind, the first five volumes, bathed in the distant light of dawn. Vol. 6: 3500–3000 BC. Still archaeology and myths, but now the walls of Jericho. Vol. 7: 3000–2500 BC. The Egyptians arrive, archaeology, myths, and historical names. Vol. 8: 2500–2000 BC. By the end of this volume we have made it halfway through human history, as viewed with our unmarred historical consciousness. Vol. 9: 2000–1500 BC. Isn't it almost time for Moses to lead the Jews out of the land of Egypt, spending forty years in the desert in order to reach the Promised Land? Yes, soon, because the history of the world has reached the halfway point now, measured with our unmarred, but terminating historical consciousness. Vol. 10: 1500–1000 BC. Now Moses appears. First as an abandoned baby in the bulrushes, then as the man who leads his people back to his Promised Land, as he sees it, yet he dies before he arrives there. In this volume Joshua's troops blow their trumpets to topple the walls of Jericho, incredibly enough four volumes after the walls appeared for the first time, newly erected. Vol. 11: 1000–500 BC; Vol. 12: 500 BC–AD 0; Vol. 13: AD 0–500. The Roman Empire has an emperor who has ruled for thirty years, called Augustus, and by the end of the volume the Western Roman Empire, Rome, has fallen, while the Eastern Roman Empire, Byzantium, still exists. Vol. 14: AD 500–1000. Midway through this volume Charlemagne is crowned emperor of the Holy Roman Empire in Aachen, while Byzantium continues to exist. Vol. 15, the next to last volume about the history of human civilization: AD 1000–1500. In this volume, toward the end, Byzantium falls. Vol. 16:

AD 1500–2000. (In reality, ending just before the French Revolution, let's say the day when Mozart wrote down the last chords of *The Marriage of Figaro*.) This is *Aschehoug's Revised History of the World*, first revision of Armand's original revision.

28B. "Vol. 16: 1800–2000 (in reality ending in 1945)" in the revised edition of *Aschehoug's History of the World* and Vol. 16: AD 1500–2000 (in reality, ending just before the French Revolution, let's say the day when Mozart wrote down the last chords of *The Marriage of Figaro*) in the revision of *Aschehoug's History of the World* (which could also be called the first alternative to the revised edition) points to a problem. When does the time end for descendants to legitimately pass judgment on the past? Armand had chosen 1945 as the line of demarcation, the stopping point for the space of time about which a man toward the end of the twentieth century has the right to speak in an overview of world history (actually European history). Even when the last volume deals with the period 1800–2000. We know too little about everything after 1945; all the research done on the period 1945–2000 must be categorized as tentative, experimental, a modest suggestion. The same holds true if the last volume, the sixteenth, deals with the period 1500–2000. But a period of five hundred years presupposes that an even stricter framework regarding statements can be made. Time then seems to run more slowly, possibly with a greater cosmological understanding. The French Revolution in 1789 will then be a natural point in time, demarcating when history becomes unresolved, unclear, as symbolized by one of Wolfgang Amadeus Mozart's *resolved* works, just prior to this, as history's preliminary conclusion.

29. With this sort of disciplined view of history in the back of his mind, Armand felt that he had won the right to maintain an uninhibited sense of curiosity toward its passage. He could devote himself to feeling amazed that history had proceeded as it had and not in some other way. Just as in the life of an individual, there are many coincidences at work. If you think about your own life, over and over again, doing a thorough job of it, you'll end up terrified about leaving your room at all, in case you make a misstep and end up in an irreparable situation. Armand still remembers the icicle that fell from the sixth floor of an apartment building in Helsinki in 1994, grazing the back of his head before it crashed to the pavement where he was walking; he can still feel the gust of air from that sudden assault, or embrace, of death. It's the same thing with the passage of history; the number of such coincidences that either strike or don't strike, though it may be a very close call, are and were endless. Armand spent a lot of time brooding over these random events, pondering whether they represented a general principle that drives history forward or just considering them as individual coincidences that particularly intrigued him. This became a favorite pastime of his. When it came right down to it, this was part of the training to which he subjected himself in order to rediscover the historical discipline that he had lost.

30. Before we even know a single person by name, what was most important had already been achieved! The horse had been tamed. The ox was hitched to the plow. The pig was in its sty. The sheep was grazing peacefully. The four seed grains were a

fact; and nothing has changed over the passage of time: no new grains have appeared. No new domestic animals have shown up! Throughout history the tiger has lived in the jungle, where it has been trapped and caught, put on display in the circus, but it has not been tamed. It still kills the animal tamer for inexplicable reasons. And the bear is still the bear roaming great distances. And the moose. Why hasn't the moose become domesticated? Couldn't the moose have been hitched to the plow with much greater effect than the ox? Then why the ox instead of the moose? Couldn't the moose be tamed? The big, long-legged moose? With its antlers? The wild moose that knows when it has been seen, shaking its antlers and sending a rushing sound through the forest, through the trees. The ox isn't as strong as the moose, yet it was the one that was tamed. The tamed ox is still furious and far more dangerous than the tamed moose would be! Why wasn't the moose tamed? Does it eat too much? But now it's too late, it would take thousands of years to tame the moose. What about the bear? Why not tame the bear? In the circus the bear can be trained to do all sorts of tricks; maybe it would take only a couple of hundred years before the bear could be tamed to become a useful domesticated animal. The bear in a sty.

---

31. Christianity's capacity for survival: it is human-made, perhaps a historical coincidence.

---

32. When Spain was a world power, their kings were addressed as "Your Catholic Majesty." During their reign—the reign of the Spanish Habsburgs—an attempt was made to influence

the Holy See in Rome to preach a new dogma: the doctrine of the double virginal birth. Not only Mary but also her mother Anna was impregnated by the Holy Spirit. Under the Catholic Kings Philip II, Philip III, Philip IV, and the imbecilic Charles (Carlos II), dispatches were constantly sent to Rome, urging the preaching of this doctrine as the true word of God. There was an obvious reason for the keen interest of the Spanish court in this matter. It offended the Spanish courtiers, and also the Spanish clergy who served the Catholic kings, that the Virgin Mary, the mother of Jesus, hadn't herself been conceived by a virgin. She was therefore defiled at birth, and it was a paradox that the Son of God should have been born to a defiled woman, even if that woman had been impregnated as a virgin by the undefiled Holy Spirit. This appeal was regularly sent to the Holy See in Rome over a period lasting one hundred and fifty years. But the Holy See never adopted the request. The doctrine of the double virginal birth never became Christian dogma. The Catholic kings had to live with this paradox. Armand fully understood their argument, which had turned out not to be sufficient for the Holy See. Armand often wondered what the Holy See's own argument had been in not adopting the urgent and persistent appeals of the Catholic kings. It was probably written down somewhere, though Armand had not yet discovered it. When he was stationed in Madrid, he made frequent visits to the Prado Museum, which houses Velázquez's paintings of the Spanish Habsburg monarchs. Velázquez portrayed all of them as deeply serious—especially Philip IV—lost in their own, perhaps deep, thoughts. There is reason to assume that Velázquez was familiar with the quibbling of the Catholic kings with regard to the Holy See in Rome, and that he therefore painted the kneeling Philip in such a way that it's clear to the viewer, this man is tormented by the thought of the defilement that has become associated with the figure of Christ, because His Holiness in Rome has not presented the necessary explanation that will erase all doubt regarding the purity of the Virgin Mary, from birth onward.

---

33. The dirigible. Around 1930 it seemed as if it had a real future. Especially carrying passengers through the air. But that's not what happened. Instead, it was the flying machine that triumphed in the battle for the peaceful territory of the air. Now, all traveling through the air takes place via machines whose direct and unmistakable forebears are the fragile flying machines of the Wright brothers. That's actually too bad. It would have done us good to see dirigibles in the sky today. It would have made the oceans of the air much livelier. Next to slender fighter planes, with their mysterious trails, the whirring helicopters, which are the insects of the air, and the commercial planes coming in for a landing over the city's rooftops (those giant metallic birds, roaring infernally as they approach the landing sites at the airports) it would have been a relief to the eye to stare upward and catch sight of a dirigible slowly sailing off, like a blue whale of the air, saved from extinction.

---

34. And otherwise: all these coincidences of history, which could have changed things drastically. The best-known example

is Julian, the Roman emperor in the fourth century who was also known as *Julian the Apostate*. And what if Pearl Harbor hadn't happened? That's another.

---

35. Armand knew the author who is writing this. Back then I wasn't an author but a student from the same town as him, two or three years older, but belonging to somewhat the same circle. We haven't met later on, but he has undoubtedly read about me in the newspapers, maybe he has even read some of my books, probably surprised that I became a communist, a member of the AKP (the Workers' Communist Party), a Maoist. That was not the path he had expected me to take. Later on, I read Armand's mature reflections on Ibsen's play *Brand*, and his thoughts were no doubt influenced by the fact that the AKP also included me, most likely to quite a high degree. Even though Armand and I were distant friends who later lost all contact with each other, it so happens that distant friends from your youth—from the time when you are just starting out and up until your midtwenties—can illuminate both your own life and the age in which you're living to a strangely significant degree; actually far more importantly than close friends can. You might call this the triumph of the minor characters, meaning that those individuals who are minor characters in real life, when everything is going on at the present moment, are able to elevate themselves to a position of main character in the pale light of reflection, after the fact.

I also knew Paul Buer; for a time we belonged to the same circle, a group of students, and we shared a background, having grown up in the same town on the west side of the Oslo

Fjord. Actually, it was Paul Buer that I was interested in for a literary project. And that's not so strange, considering his tragic end. But it turned out to be Armand instead, maybe because of the indecipherable nature of his life, seen from my point of view. But it's clear that Paul Buer's life still interests me—the way he involuntarily flung himself onto a path which required him to respond, with great seriousness, with all of his "self," to what for him was an incredible and aimless schism between the truth (in his terminology: scientific facts) and the State, something which for him resulted in fateful—meaning in the final instance, irretrievable—consequences, and this still incites my literary interest, even my conscience, not to mention literary passion. Maybe I have faith that I will end my work as an author with a novel at least dedicated to his memory, and, if I can find the courage, to his life.

———————

36. Historical coincidences vs. historical necessities. Is it out of necessity that we proceed the way we do? That seems to be how it is. We can deduce this from two things. First, what exists seems immutable. But of course that's not true. History presents many examples of the opposite, but when the opposite occurs, it's easy to point to factors that caused the immutable to crack and a chasm to be revealed, so that the opposite of the immutable came into view and became a historical fact. For instance, the Soviet Union. When the Soviet Union collapsed, it wasn't hard to point to why things happened the way they did. It was even easier to wonder why it hadn't happened earlier. But prior to the collapse of the Soviet Union, for example in

1985, no one predicted the Soviet Union would collapse, that seemed unthinkable, and no one wanted to tarnish their own reputation by publicly expressing the idea that the Soviet Union would soon collapse, except through a nuclear war (which they would have lost).

Second, what exists can be proven, meaning that it's easy to explain why it is what it is, and not something else. We can explain historical development, and we can deny it only by means of speculations in which we don't really believe. And what does this mean? It means that even if we don't study our own time, we still have to submit to it. That's what is immutable, and a fact, with all it comprises, signifying our perspective on time itself. We have to submit to it because for us there is no other time to which we can relate. Even Galileo had to surrender to his own time. He declared himself defeated by his contemporaries and renounced his theories as false. The reason was not only that he feared being judged and burned at the stake as a heretic, but he also feared that the rulers of his day had better arguments than he did. What do I say to this? That I too, confronted with the rulers, may be forced to withdraw my opinions, and do so quite voluntarily. Or keep them to myself.

(signed) Armand V., Norwegian diplomat

––––––––––

37. It's true, that old story about how the wings of a butterfly on Tahiti can set off a hurricane in the North Atlantic. How impressive it is that they've come up with this incredible, even unlikely, story. It's called meteorology. Fact after fact, over hundreds of years. It's not so strange that they're wrong about

tomorrow's weather, given how many butterfly wings there are, how many things there are in general. Of course today it's not possible to measure that sort of influence with precision, but just *knowing* about it affects our prediction or understanding of what the weather will be like tomorrow. If mistakes are made—and that's always going to happen given what we know in our epoch—it will be at least partially because of such things as the butterflies—not their unpredictability, but our inability (up until now) to calculate the extent of this predictability, of butterfly wings, the whole world's butterfly-wing predictability at the exact tenth of a second (or even less, the same millionth of a second, and subsequently, in the name of precision, at an even smaller fraction of time, etc., etc., etc., etc.) next to equally impossible things, such as the bending of blades of grass, the swaying of flowers (as well as other things, the bark of trees, the mold in the underlying soil, I could go on forever, until I end up creating a clear sky over the Hallingskarvet mountain range). That's what Armand would have said on that day in the late 1990s when he received a visit from Paul Buer at his private residence in the embassy in Madrid.

———

38. Does Armand's gaze reveal his seriousness? Not when he looks at the world. Or at others. But what if Armand's gaze turns inward? It's possible. It's possible that Armand's gaze may be turned inward, and that he then sees the seriousness that "is," but that cannot be reached. Does the fact that it can't be reached mean that it's ineffable and beyond our understanding? Can I then say that this gaze is unbearable? That it peers into

itself and catches sight of what is unbearable? After the usual phases of a human life have been lived?

———

39. "What remains after the usual phases of a human life have been lived?" What do I mean by that? That which is left after childhood, adolescence, manhood, and old age have all been lived, and an essence has crystallized? That which "is" Armand? Armand's essence? The gaze of the sixty-three-year-old Armand. Is that the essence? The man who looks at others? At the world? "This is an attempt to express the dreamlike unreality of the time—beyond everything truly serious—that can never be reached, what remains after the usual phases of a human life have been lived." Found among the notes. Two separate notes, written down independently of each other, but by the same person. It has to be the gaze. The aging man's gaze. The gaze of the man who wrote these two notes, independent of each other.

———

40. His own death made him thoughtful. But more than his own inevitable fate he feared the future of humankind. To behold the dreamlike, fragmentary inactivity, beyond everything truly serious, that's what is left after the usual phases of a human life have been lived.

40 B. "But more than his own inevitable fate he feared the future of humankind." It's difficult for me to chance a regular comma here, actually it's simply impossible, so if it's possible, I ask to be spared.

41. It's true, that meteorological story about a butterfly's wings on Tahiti setting off a hurricane in the North Atlantic. How impressive that humanity has come up with this incredible, even unlikely story that is called meteorology. Fact after fact over hundreds of years. Not so strange that they're wrong about tomorrow's weather, given how many butterflies there are, how many things there are in general.

Of course today it's not possible to measure that sort of influence with precision, but just *knowing* about it puts meteorology in its true perspective. If they're wrong about the weather on a specific tomorrow—and they will continue to be wrong, given what we know in our epoch—it won't be because of the butterflies' unpredictability, but because of our inability to calculate countless unpredictabilities next to equally impossible things, such as the bending of blades of grass, the swaying of flowers, the peace of the forest.

42. It was his voice, or his way of speaking. It had fundamentally changed, he was certain of that, even though he hadn't met, or spoken to, Paul Buer in more than twenty-five years. When he saw the list of the Norwegian representatives at the meteorological world congress in Madrid that year, he was pleased to find Paul Buer's name, and it was with an almost childish joy that he signed the invitation to the reception at the embassy. He felt this way because it's always with great anticipation that we meet an old friend again after so many years, but also because he was happy that Paul Buer was part of the Norwegian delegation;

that meant he couldn't have been thrown out of the professional community, as he had suspected might happen, and as he had feared. Armand hadn't heard much about Paul Buer over the past few years, but he knew that he'd been extremely involved in some meteorological measurements being done in connection with whether Oslo's new main airport should be built in Hurum, Gardermoen, or Hobøl, and he seemed to have discovered some errors, irregularities, or even chicanery that was of decisive importance when it came to choosing Gardermoen in the end. When the Norwegian delegates arrived for the reception, Armand immediately recognized Paul Buer and smiled to himself as he looked forward to welcoming him. Certainly he had changed, but that was only natural, he was now a man in his fifties, so it was a slightly faltering version of Paul Buer he now saw, a more stooped version, stiffer and slower than the person he had known, but no doubt the same can be said of me, Armand thought, because the basic features are the same for both Paul and me. He shook Paul Buer's hand, holding on to it for a long time as he allowed his joy to overflow at this reunion. But Paul Buer responded in a superficial and formal manner. Armand was astonished; didn't Paul Buer recognize him by his appearance, or hadn't it sunk in that the Norwegian ambassador's name was identical to the name of his old childhood friend? Not wanting to startle him by exclaiming: But don't you recognize me? he said instead: "How many years has it been since we last met?" And Paul Buer replied: "Exactly twenty-six years." He was taken aback by the tone of Paul's voice, and his surprise continued as he exchanged more words with him. His voice had fundamentally changed, and that put Armand on guard. The rhythm of his phrasing had no connection with the man who was speaking, it had no social connection, or consideration, there was no question about that, it was a fact. And he also spoke too loudly, as if he weren't hearing his own voice or it wasn't actually his. I need to make sure I don't favor him over the other meteorologists just because he's an old friend, thought Armand, so he turned to the man next to Paul Buer and got wrapped up in a joking discussion of the weather with him, since they were after all (as he pointed out) delegates at an international meteorological conference. But Paul Buer remained standing there next to his colleague instead of continuing into the reception area as the others who had been introduced before him had done, and he joined in with the joking discussion by making a couple of conventional statements about the weather in general, again spoken in that too-loud but extremely formal manner.

Armand deftly wound up his welcoming remarks with Paul Buer's colleague and then turned to the man standing next to him, and Paul Buer's colleague moved on into the room. Fortunately Paul Buer then realized that he too should move on and not stand there taking up space, so to speak, while his old friend, the present Norwegian envoy to Spain, greeted his guests arriving for the reception.

Later, no opportunity presented itself for a private conversation with Paul Buer. Armand was the host, with a host's obligations. Certainly he had hoped that there would be occasion for the two old friends, who'd known each other in their youth, to have even just a few minutes alone, but such an occasion didn't arise, even though Armand was on the lookout for just such an occasion. Yet it can't be denied that the brief introductory meeting of the two men had made Armand deeply concerned about the state of his old friend. This was reinforced over the course of the reception. Again and again he heard Paul Buer's voice rise above the others' in a staccato and obstinate manner, even though what he said didn't require the least obstinacy, but was part of an ordinary and easy-flowing conversation, which the rhythm of Paul Buer's phrasing destroyed. His whole being and manner were colored by this staccato and obstinate voice, such that Paul Buer no longer made a good impression on those around him, though he had undeniably done so before, back when they were young students. Armand felt a jolt of sadness pass through him every time he, immersed as he was in easy conversations with others, heard his old friend's disconnected voice slice through the air of the room, even from the far end of it. That is a man in need, he thought. That is a man trapped in his own battle for justice and truth. Nothing else matters to him anymore. The truth has become an internal obsession, everything else he does takes place outside his control, or interest. He has lost control. Or interest in having any control over external reality. The only thing with any effect on external reality is that the truth should make inroads there, so that reality can be restored, become whole again. Armand heard Paul Buer's voice wherever he went. He tried again to find an occasion to speak to him alone, if only for a few minutes, so that their reunion might cause him, he hoped, to fall back to his natural tone of voice from the time before Paul Buer was knocked down by some chicanery that nobody wanted to change. But the closest he came to this was sitting at a small table over coffee and cognac, together with a group that included Paul Buer. Then he exchanged a few words with him, and he had to listen to Paul Buer talking to him with that same staccato and obstinate voice, which had apparently now become permanent. Even when he uttered some banal comment about how cognac was not something he drank every day, the tone of voice in which the words were spoken could easily be interpreted as a slightly tactless criticism of the debauchery practiced in the private residence of this Norwegian embassy, instead of a cheerful expression of contentment at being able to, once in a while, step beyond everyday parameters to enjoy sips of this noble elixir. But he must at least have retained his professional status, thought Armand. Otherwise he wouldn't be here, as a delegate to this conference. In spite of everything.

When the reception was finally over and it was time for the guests to take their leave from the evening's host, including Paul Buer, Armand again shook his hand, this time to say goodbye, and he seized the opportunity to ask Paul Buer whether he might join him for lunch the next day. But Paul Buer said that he couldn't. By then the conference would have started, and every minute would be filled. This reception was only possible because it was held the day before the conference began, on the very evening when the Norwegian delegates arrived in Madrid.

"But I could possibly decline an invitation to an official event on Thursday evening," Paul Buer added, in his unsettling and unwavering voice.

"I'm afraid that I'm busy that evening, and unfortunately it's not an invitation I can decline," replied Armand, sadly.

---

43. Here we'll break in to insert ourselves in a footnote that diverges from the chronological course of events. At this point in the novel up above, or in the text out there, which is actually

complete and can only be landed like a fish, Paul Buer has long since met his end. When this happened, it caused no ripple in the text down here, the real text, the one that will shine in the end.

But now a ripple does occur, at a point that has nothing to do with Paul Buer, but which still has to do with his demise. When Armand V. got the news of Paul Buer's passing, you couldn't really say that he was surprised. His first reaction was to wonder whether he should have done more to arrange a private meeting with him that time in Madrid. Paul himself had not been unwilling; he had even suggested that he could cancel an invitation to another event on that Thursday so he could meet with Armand. But Armand couldn't make it, it was absolutely impossible. That is, it would have been possible under one specific condition. Meaning if he'd been afraid that if he didn't meet Paul Buer on that Thursday evening, it would spell his end; if he had been so sure of this, he could have used it as a candid justification for canceling an arrangement that could not be called off except under utterly extraordinary circumstances. But this wasn't the situation, not at that time, and not now either, just a few months later, now that it's known that Paul Buer's tragic demise had occurred. And even if Armand might have suspected that Paul Buer would meet his tragic fate only a few months later, would having dinner in Madrid with him have possibly altered in any way what was about to happen? No. No doubt it was regrettable that nothing came of any dinner with the two of them; after all these years, it might have been good for both of them, it might even have turned into an evening full of the joy of reconnecting; but in terms of what happened, it would have had no effect whatsoever. *That* was determined by something else entirely.

And Armand knew it. That's why Armand took the news of Paul Buer's demise in stride. But he was shaken, and he pondered a good deal about what sort of powers had gathered in Paul Buer's mind and had been ravaging there in the final years of his life. Everything points to the fact that Paul Buer had not expected to be ignored when he was able to present clear proof that there'd been chicanery with the meteorological data in conjunction with the politics regarding where the future main airport for Oslo should be located. It didn't matter to Paul Buer whether the airport was to be located in Gardermoen or Hurum, but when he had discovered an obvious technical error that could have catastrophic consequences for the decision-making process if it was not pointed out and corrected, he considered it his duty to speak up. He couldn't understand it when he was ignored, and when he did at last understand it, he could not accept it. It went against everything he'd believed this society was based on, and from then on nothing mattered to him other than truth, justice, and the restoration of the old order Paul Buer had lived by as a natural fundamental principle. Viewed in this way, it is far from certain that a private dinner with Paul Buer that time in Madrid would have been any sort of edifying affair; for that to happen, it would have to be presupposed that the professional diplomat, Armand, succeeded in directing the conversation smoothly toward topics other than this grievance which had struck Paul Buer in his battle for truth and justice, and in the best case it would have resulted in a couple of hours' relief for Paul Buer from his agitated state of mind; and that would have been worth it, we can say in hindsight, but whether it could have saved Paul Buer's life has to be ruled out, or almost ruled out. Yet if only he could have managed, Armand thought, to see Paul calm down even for a brief moment, and experience a moment of tranquility, oh yes, he would have given a lot to see that happen, but that was an impossible thought, from first to last, both the idea that they could have had dinner together, the two of them, back then in Madrid, and that the dinner might have unfolded as Armand now fantasized about the way it could have gone.

————

44. He'd thought a lot about Paul Buer after the reception in Madrid, and about the fact that Paul had been weighed down from being a witness to the truth, and to such an extent that he'd lost his social voice, the one we all need in order to be around others. Although it had pained him to see Paul in this state, and although he had some idea, even back then in Madrid, that his condition was caused by some matter that had marked him so strongly that Armand suspected it was about to spell his demise, which in fact did happen a few months later, he never took the step to find out about the specific matter, even though it would have been entirely possible since the documents were in the public record, as well as any counterarguments. He could have formed his own opinion about the matter, but he didn't. Why not? Maybe because that's just not something anyone does, and maybe because if Armand had done so, he would have had an unpleasant feeling that he was scrutinizing another man, an old friend, poking around in his papers, and doing so when nobody had asked him to. I think that's the way it was. Armand can at least say as much with confidence, and there are no more questions to ask.

45. But if he had eaten dinner with him back then in Madrid (which had proved impossible) and he'd heard Paul talk with great intensity, and much too loudly, as Armand must have figured he would, tirelessly, tirelessly, to the point of annoyance, and Armand had then suggested that Paul should explain the whole matter, what then? It's an impossible thought because the dinner was impossible, because it could have taken place only under circumstances that were not in place, because Armand couldn't have foreseen Paul Buer's demise, and even if he might have had some suspicion, that suspicion wasn't strong or convincing enough for him to openly act on that suspicion, or fear, to cancel one of the inviolable obligations of his official position, scheduled for that very same evening. But couldn't he have contacted Paul later? Sent him a letter suggesting that he would look into the matter and eventually offer him, Paul Buer, some advice? Yes, he might have done that. But during the reception at the embassy, Paul hadn't mentioned even a single word about the matter. So Armand remained clueless.

46. No one can accuse another person, even when it comes to a best friend, of not taking it upon himself to decide to carry out an independent investigation in a matter that is clearly proving to be a torment. Yet it still nagged at Armand that he hadn't done so. Even though he was greatly concerned about Paul Buer's fate, both before and after his tragic demise, it's a fact that he didn't have the slightest inkling of the proof that Paul claimed he had in his possession and that was never taken

seriously by those who should have taken it seriously. He never investigated the proof that Paul said he had presented, nor did he try to track down the counterarguments to which those in charge resorted when they chose not to take his proof seriously, nor did he try to find out how the alleged suppression of Paul Buer's true revelations had taken place in practice. He retained his memory of Buer as someone passionate about the truth, his truth, to the extent that it spelled his demise. But he refused to investigate the actual state of things. He had his reasons for this. Because if Armand had looked into this matter that was so vital to Buer, with the intention of verifying it and seeking the truth, what would he have found? That Buer's proof was without question correct, as Buer himself had believed so steadfastly that he'd even lost his social voice out of sheer horror that no one was willing to listen to his documented proof of the truth? That was not what Armand would have wanted. If this was the truth, then he didn't want to know about it. The mere idea that Buer's proof might have needed a more thorough verification kept him from taking a look at those documents. He didn't want to remember Buer in any other way than he now remembered him. The lost man in Madrid, the man eaten up from the inside by the truth because it wasn't allowed to be released but was instead forced into a restrictive exile inside of him.

_____

47. Armand had gone home to attend Paul Buer's funeral. He came up with an appropriate reason for going to Oslo for consultations with the foreign ministry so that he'd be able to show up for the funeral of his old friend. But when he arrived at the

Vestre Gravlund cemetery and slowly walked toward the chapel of the crematorium and caught sight of a group of nicely dressed people, both women and men, clustered outside the chapel, he stopped. He was struck with a great sense of loneliness, because he realized that he shouldn't be there. He couldn't make himself continue on toward the group, so he had no choice but to turn around. He walked along the pathways in the cemetery and heard the chapel bells toll at the start of the service for Paul Buer. He wandered around nearby during the whole funeral, and when the chapel bells again tolled, he was standing at the edge of the parking lot, watching the mourners come out of the chapel.

----

48. That was a long time ago now. But every once in a while Armand would think about it again. Suddenly it would pop into his mind, and since he made no attempt to push the thought aside, there it was again, and he would replay everything in his mind one more time. He couldn't simply push it aside, he had decided that was something he couldn't do, out of consideration for his deceased old friend. It's a way of showing him respect, thought Armand, and I'll just have to bear the brunt of it. And one more time he'd think about the matter, about the documents he'd never investigated. Even though it had been virtually impossible for him to suggest to Buer in a natural way—for example via a letter, after the reception in Madrid—that he would take a look at the documentation in order to reach his own opinion, which might have offered some support to his hard-pressed childhood friend, it wasn't *entirely* impossible to do this after Buer passed away. Of course you might say that this would no

longer have any meaning, but for Armand V. himself it would have meant something to be able to undertake an assessment of whether there was any relevance to Buer's documentation of chicanery in the matter of the main airport. But he didn't do anything about it. He refused, and he knew why. Because what if he had indeed gone through the documents and discovered that Buer was right? What would the consequences have been for Armand? Wouldn't he then have had to speak up? Loudly, so everybody heard? Publicly? Write letters and approach those who were in charge? In short, he would have had to become Buer's ally in his battle for the truth. While Buer was still alive. Or to become, at the very least, his posthumous ally, after his death, speaking up in a resounding voice. Yes, he would have been obligated to do that, it was something he couldn't have easily avoided. There was no way to avoid it, except by not investigating what the whole matter was about. Certainly, he didn't want to appear to be Buer's ally. His whole being had resisted doing that, and it still did. Again he pictured the way Buer had looked that time in Madrid. He recalled his obstinate voice. It had seemed so unpleasant. He'd found it horrifying. He so wished he could have done something for him, but he could not join his cause. Not even when, or if, Paul had truth on his side. He should have done it, if Buer had been right in pointing out that some chicanery had occurred, a false meteorological measurement, that had crucial importance for the decision-making process, and hence was suppressed, greeted with suspicion; if in fact Paul's judgment had been smeared, slandered, he'd been met with distortions, half-truths, bureaucratic pretexts, maybe even outright lies. But Armand couldn't do it. It went against the grain; Buer's reality was not his. The reality of the wronged individual went against the grain for Armand. He couldn't share in the situation of the wronged individual, even though that person was right and represented Truth and the order that needed to be restored. Armand was too bound to his own position as a diplomat. He liked the ways of diplomacy, which were as far from Buer's ways as they could possibly be. There was something about the ease of diplomacy, in associating with others, in conventions and codes, that spoke more strongly to him than he'd so far ever imagined. It was the civilized nature of the diplomatic ways, which also served as its basis and genesis, to which he now felt so drawn, and which also, when it came right down to it, was Armand's anchor that he cast into the deep whenever he had to explain his own life. And it resisted the figure of Paul Buer, that person who had recklessly continued on toward his own downfall, with all his sense of injustice, all his fanaticism on behalf of the Truth.

This was what Armand now acknowledged. He would give a great deal not to have come to this acknowledgment. This was the worst possibility. That he hadn't investigated Buer's documentation because he'd feared his old friend was right. That he was right and had been opposed by powerful forces that didn't want Buer's proof to make it onto the agenda. This is the truth. It was many years ago now since Buer passed away. Yet Armand V., the Norwegian diplomat, still wandered around Oslo, pondering these agonies.

---

49. To repeat: Armand was intent on living a noble life. Serve his country? Serve God? Serve society? Without these sorts of questions Armand would not exist, even though he would have

answered every one of them with "no." But Armand exists because these questions exist in his consciousness, even though they should have been answered long ago, in the negative. He called this having a civilized consciousness. His denial does not comprise a denial of the questions. What he means is that it makes little difference whether there's a light at the end of the tunnel or not. It's more important to look for an escape hatch, a way out of the whole thing, somewhere or other within the tunnel. But what may astonish an outsider is the elegance and malice with which this man can behave, he who is really only looking for a way out of the whole thing.

49 B . What is actually meant by an escape hatch in the tunnel? Think about a tunnel. A mountain tunnel. Where is the escape hatch there? As far as we know, nowhere; if there *is* a hatch it's in any case not an escape hatch. Imagine another tunnel. A tunnel underwater. Where is the escape hatch there (the water gushes in, you could call it the deluge, but it's hardly an escape hatch)? Or are you picturing the road tunnels *underground*? Then the escape hatch would have to be an exit ramp, clearly marked. A clearly marked road out of the underground passage, in spite of everything. Does that make sense? Hardly. This is what Armand might have been thinking about, sitting on the edge of the bed, as he took off his diplomatic suit after a long day at the office, or after a reception, or after a fairly confidential meeting.

—————

50. Now that Armand was basically waiting around for his last assignment—the one that would take him to London or Paris,

and that he called his Crowning Achievement—he occasionally suffered from sudden dizziness. It might happen at any moment, but especially when he was at the foreign ministry on Victoria Terrace. An acute dizziness which, while it lasted, made him consider going to see a doctor—a thought that he would again brush aside, or at least postpone, as soon as the dizzy spell subsided. He knew what it was. It was sheer anxiety, and he knew why. It had to do with the fact that he was unable to identify with anything related to his job, except for the outward arrangements he was constantly obliged to undertake. He merely put on a good show. He didn't mean a word he said, nor did he stand wholeheartedly behind anything he did. It was all mimicry. When others were upset, Armand was upset too. When they were proud of what the foreign ministry had managed to accomplish, when it had to do with national security, peace processes around the world, negotiations, influence, etc., etc., and they all enthusiastically exclaimed with genuine esprit de corps, then Armand would also play along, if need be.

———————

51. At this very moment, on his way home in the car, a random thought occurred to him, or as he described it to himself: something I don't yet even dare think about. If our time is viewed from the outside, from the viewpoint of the future and not the past, what will they say? About hangers-on like Armand V.? Each time such thoughts appeared, he rejected them without argument. The argumentation came later, when such a thought didn't merely cross his mind, rather he knew it by heart, though that didn't mean it was bad or wrong.

52. Toward the end of his embassy assignments in service to the Norwegian state, Armand V. had to conclude: our lineage has gotten away from this. It's impossible to look the truth in the eye. This has gone too far. There's no way back.

53. Even for him, the diplomat, it was difficult to understand what had happened. It was a radical transformation, which might be exciting, it ought to be, at any rate, for our Armand, but it was mostly frightening.

54. "You shouldn't make such a fuss," said Armand. But the person he was talking to showed no remorse. Not at the time.

55. The fact that our country's female defense minister—in the new millennium our country's defense minister we will be female—embraces the world leader's chief war representative isn't anything special from an international perspective. The nomenclature of small countries tends to require that, thought Armand. He laughed. The difference is simply that for the governments of other small countries, this is necessary in order to retain power, meaning to obtain the protection of the world's leader against your own people. Not so here. He laughed again. The gleeful Norwegian diplomat, who wandered around Oslo, waiting for his appointment to Paris or London, his crowning achievement. (Why not Washington?)

56. It may be that, no matter what, it wasn't possible. And this can't be blamed on Armand V. The cause may lie in the very speed with which the journey proceeds, erasing all hope that the questions that should be asked, are asked. On that evening Armand had a clear sense that he saw everything, all his desires, both in the past and the future, in one vision, which made him double over, as if in pain. All those desires, which we pay for with our peace of mind: vanity, the desire to be seen. There. Up there. But "up there," from the plan's point of view, is not up there in the novel, fate's point of view, but it can be described only here. Here. Down here. This vision came to Armand right after he had yet again visited his son and was on his way home. They'd had a long conversation in which he, the father, had taken a peremptory tone. In addition to pain, he also felt a strong urge to radically transform what he had seen, give it a shake, turn it upside down, if for no other reason than to express his mute protest. But Armand belongs here. In the world of symbols. From the point of view of speed. Together with all the others parading, intoxicated with vanity, around what is invisible (power). People clothe themselves in importance, as representatives, as highly visible, even behind closed doors. The Visible: themselves, glitzy, flashy, in the spotlight, under the glitter of the myriad crystals in the chandelier. Media people, TV stars, ambassadors, ministers, all of them operating with the intoxication of vanity, in a circle around the Void, the invisibility of power, and they want to be seen that way, or seen as they enter the inner sanctum, knowing that the doors will be closed solemnly behind them, that's where they go to catch a

glimpse of the Void, the Invisible (power)—that which moves, that which has consequences, that which is immovable.

―――――

57. Perhaps what I mean is Armand's hopelessness. Armand's fundamental lack of hope. What does Armand have instead of hope? Don't know. But: no sense of destiny, a lack of purpose, the fact that Armand has no plan, no Armand-plan that makes a novel about him readable, or writable, are descriptions that immediately come to mind, unbidden, when Armand's fundamental lack of hope, his hopelessness, presents itself. Regardless of whether he serves his country or not; and that is what he does, of course, whether he wants to or not, and on its terms, not his own. Watch out that you don't lose your inner cheerfulness, which is your soul. All your achievements.

―――――

58. The fact that Norway can get bigger by joining the EU is, for many who are part of his milieu and his profession, a fascinating, even glitzy idea. It's the only thing that can get us into the History of the World. Outside of it, we are, and will continue to be, a province, as we've always been. For the most part a colony to a third-rate, possibly fourth-rate power (Denmark). The dream of Norway as a major power goes through the EU. This was something the diplomat Armand V. knew. And he shrugged.

   This megalomania among the country's leading forces was not becoming to the nation. Rather, it was destructive. The case of Greenland in the late 1920s now had a follow-up. Norwegian megalomania is not pretty (even though relatively speaking it's utterly harmless, bearing in mind the Greenland case, and the Olympics in Lillehammer).

———————

59. Even for him, the diplomat, it was difficult to understand what had happened. This was a radical transformation that might be exciting, at least it ought to be, for our Armand, but it was mostly frightening.

———————

60. For many reasons Armand could not, even for himself, effect a consistent criticism of America and America's behavior in the world. Not even in his own mind. But he knew this, and he didn't hesitate to make it known that he knew, in his own mind.

———————

61. Now and then, such as right here, it's possible to have an odd feeling, almost like déjà vu, that you're on some forgotten trip. As this is being written, did Armand find himself on a street in Prague? Something tells us that it might seem that way. Is it Josefov, formerly the Jewish quarter in Prague, this refers to, with all its narrow confines, the sudden curving of the street pattern, and the big restaurant whose door opens right off the street, after the roadway has straightened out again?

———————

62. Scratched on. Some obscure scratching, as if on the fetal membrane. Signs that cannot be deciphered, but are there. The

night shows that they are there, when the factories of dreams whir and drone. The dream pipes steam, the products are unclear, but true, and much in demand by the person who awakes afterward, completely out of it.

———————

63. The state prison in Ohio. A murderer is going to be executed. A last request. A cigarette. Denied.

63B. There's probably no reason to feel sympathy for this murderer. Yet when you ask, nevertheless, if he has a last request, and he wants a cigarette, surely he could have had one, since you did ask him if he had a last request, just before he's going to be executed.

———————

64. The vision of a Universe without life. Endless, silent—like a beautiful thought. God's thought, in contrast to the History of the World. In contrast, of course, to the globe on which we live, where God, according to our religion, sent his Son, his only child, to be crucified, to save us, as atonement for our sins. Where is Armand now? He's nowhere in sight. Not even here in the footnotes of his life.

———————

65. All these footnotes seem to be suffering from one thing or another. The footnotes are suffering. The unwritten novel appears as heaven. In reality, there's no heaven, and the footnotes are not its hell. But the footnotes are suffering.

66. Armand's second wife showed up in the early 1980s and became the mother of his son. She was fiddling with a key ring at the front entrance to a big apartment complex on Oslo's west side when Armand came past. The key ring held a number of keys, probably a dozen in all, and it seemed as though she wasn't sure which was the correct key for this particular lock. So Armand offered his assistance. She handed him the key ring, and after glancing at the dozen keys, Armand chose one, stuck it in the lock, and turned it. The door opened as he cautiously pushed, and he held it open for her as he handed back the key ring. She thanked him, told him her untranslatable name, and went inside.

67. A man who loves a woman with an untranslatable name can become strongly attached to her. Armand's second wife showed up around 1980, they were married in 1984, and when Armand was appointed ambassador to Jordan in 1985, she went with him and moved into the residence in the Norwegian embassy as the ambassador's wife. Their son was conceived there, in the dusty city called Amman on the east bank of the Jordan river, but he was born in Norway because his mother went back there before his birth. At his birth he had a half sister, and later he grew up with another half sister five years younger than him. Armand's second marriage didn't last long.

68. Right before the birth of his son, Armand showed up in Oslo in connection with an official visit to his homeland that

had been planned well in advance so it would coincide with the big event, and he was present at the birth. However, his duties soon called him back to Amman, and he left Oslo the day after mother and child came home from the maternity clinic, returning to the apartment they had in Oslo.

---

69.   A month after the birth, Armand's second wife went back to Amman with the child. At the airport they were met by a chauffeur-driven car from the Norwegian embassy; Armand was unable to pick them up in person, but he'd made sure to outfit the car with an official Norwegian flag on both sides of the front, so that they were given a high-class welcome. This was probably not officially sanctioned, but Armand was so looking forward to their arrival that he wanted to make some small gesture, even if against regulations, to welcome the new citizen of the world and his mother. The car took them straight to the Norwegian ambassador's residence, where the child's mother was the ambassador's wife, and that same evening she would preside over a dinner that was to take place there. This became the introduction to the pattern that would characterize their marriage. Armand, who was then stationed in Amman, would later be transferred to Belgrade, and his wife would travel back and forth to these selfsame outposts of the Norwegian foreign ministry with her young son. At the airport (in Amman, later Belgrade), she would be met by an official, chauffeur-driven car, and Armand often was unable to be there, so she would be quickly taken to the ambassador's residence where she presided over official functions whenever she was at her husband's side, though when she

was back home in Norway, there were no problems of protocol because she was not present. Their son had a nanny, and sometimes Armand's wife would take trips without her young son, which Armand regarded as her soul's expression for her restless moods. These trips without her son were often combined with a trip to London or Paris, but when she returned to Amman (or Belgrade), she seemed lighthearted and would immediately resume her role as the ambassador's wife with the greatest ease. Yet, when Armand was halfway through his assignment as the Norwegian ambassador in Belgrade and was actually looking forward to spending some time at the foreign ministry back home in Oslo, they ended up separating. Of course the novel up there attempts to explain why their marriage failed. But not here. Here it is simply over. No comment. Armand missed her restless traveling, which he still today regards as the movement of a beautiful soul back and forth to him. She returned to Oslo, quickly found herself another husband (a trace of whom can be read in footnote 66), came full circle, got pregnant, and gave birth to a daughter. Since then the relationship between her and Armand has been tolerably good, out of consideration for their son, who throughout his childhood often visited his father, either by vacationing with him in Norway or by spending a certain amount of time at the foreign service stations where his father was the Norwegian envoy. In the past few years Armand hasn't seen her, since his son moved out and rented a room.

––––––––––

70. In the invisible novel you might imagine—at least I do— that if the lines to which this footnote refers had been dug up

and excavated, several sentences would now make an appearance with an entirely different tone, an entirely different sense
of drama or despair, even suppressed emotions, different from
what is expressed in the plain entry of this footnote, where I
now quite simply state that certainly a momentous event occurred in Armand V.'s life, and at a late date, after he'd turned
sixty in any case. In the unwritten text a message appears, cen-
trally placed and impossible to ignore, and this footnote is a
necessary reminder; the expressions in this footnote, which
may occasionally be mistaken for an event, have to be seen as
referring to the initial event, the unwritten one, about which we
don't know enough, because in this novel it has been denied, or
refused, it has been dug up and excavated.

---

71. This is cryptic. Much too cryptic. Not unthinkable, but unwritable. So as not to be borne. It cannot stand the light of day.

---

72. The old widow was approaching eighty. Gradually Armand
realized that she was of sound mind, but malicious. Now she
was sitting in the kitchen, talking with the other renter, a student, which is also what Armand thought his son had been.
Armand sat down at the kitchen table, picked up his briefcase,
opened it, and took out a bundle of banknotes—the monthly
rent for his son's room—which he handed to the old widow,
who greedily accepted the money, carefully counting the bills
and entering the amount in the son's rental account book,
which Armand handed to the widow so she could sign for the
payment.

After that she continued to admonish the young student, who was her renter, about how to use the kitchen in a home where he had access by virtue of his position as a renter. About keeping it clean. About the virtue of keeping it clean. About the appearance of the dish brush and the hook on the inside of a closed cupboard. About food scraps. About soap. S-O-A-P. Armand sat there spellbound, listening to her. He couldn't tear himself away. But suddenly the door to his son's room opened and out stepped his son. He had on his uniform and seemed perfectly at ease.

---

73. His son was wearing his uniform because he would soon be going back to his camp. He'd been in the military now for eight months, and in that time Armand had seen him only a few times. Now he joined his son in his room.

"Give me a call the next time you're in Oslo on leave," said Armand, "so I can take you out for a nice dinner, that would be pleasant. Do you know when you'll be back?"

His son said that he didn't know, but he would phone when he found out so they could go out to a restaurant together when he came to Oslo; he too thought that would be pleasant. The son sat down on the edge of the bed, while his father took a seat on a straight-backed chair. Armand asked how things were going with his family, and the son told him. After that a short pause ensued while they both searched for what to say next. Suddenly the son said that he really liked being in the military, much better than he'd imagined beforehand. In fact, he liked it so much that he was thinking about staying on after his compulsory military service was over in two or three months.

"What do you mean?" asked his father.

"I mean that I'm considering enlisting in a special unit," replied the son.

"A special unit?" repeated his father. "Does that mean you're thinking of signing on as an elite soldier?"

"Yes," replied the son as he sat there on the edge of the bed in his room, his back ramrod straight.

————

74. It was his father's scorn that decided the matter. If his son hadn't been subjected to that, it most likely would have remained only a fleeting idea that popped into his head and then disappeared with a slight buzzing sound. Maybe it was already only a distant buzzing when he told his father about it; at any rate it was probably just something he was playing with in his imagination, and it amused him now to say it out loud in Armand's presence. But when his father reacted with scorn, he decided to make it happen. From then on he could not be deterred. A short time later he signed a contract to become a professional soldier.

————

75. *The son decides to become an elite soldier.*

Why did Armand react with scorn toward his son even though he knew it might have consequences that would be the very opposite of what he wished on his son's behalf? Because he wasn't thinking clearly at the moment he began expressing his scorn? He, the diplomat, lost his temper when his own son told him that he was thinking of enlisting to be an elite soldier. Honestly?

The professional diplomat behaves undiplomatically toward his own son, and subsequently the son makes a choice that he probably wouldn't have made if he had not been upset by his father's undiplomatic reaction. Honestly? Let's put it this way: Armand chose to lose his temper when his son told him about this unfortunate choice he was thinking of making. He chose to lose his temper and behave as the person he was. The boy's father. He could have avoided this. He could have controlled himself. But he didn't. He was who he was. Now his son would have to become who he was going to be. If his son wanted to be a soldier, he would be a soldier. Armand quite openly scorned his own son. If other people had been present, he would have done exactly the same thing. Openly scorned him. Out in the kitchen the old widow and a young student, the other renter, sat at the table. Maybe they heard Armand V. speaking to his son in a loud and agitated voice. The son replied so quietly to everything his father said that they could hardly hear his voice, just the silence after Armand's loud tirades, a silence that lasted a minute or so, until he started up again, sounding as agitated as before. The old widow looked at the young student. The young student looked with embarrassment at the floor. The old widow caught his eye, and he nodded toward the closed door of the room where the renter, the soldier, was having a visit from his father, the diplomat.

———

76. There can hardly be any doubt that Armand washed his hands of his son and turned him into a professional soldier. He also knew full well what sort of elite forces his son would be joining. He also knew what sort of assignments were intended for special forces of that kind, outside the country's borders.

That was why he scorned his son. Scorned the very fabric of war, scorned the whole makeup of war. For once the son was given a glimpse of the thoughts stirring behind Armand's brow, now expressed with such vehemence. The son was very surprised by his father, the ambassador who had never behaved like this toward him before. The scorn couldn't help but sting, even though it wasn't personal but directed at the system that we're all part of, his father as well, in his position as a trusted government official. His father scorned the new warriors as cowardly dogs, and this included of course, and above all, his own son if he should make good on his fatal desire to join this system as an enlisted soldier whose exclusive task was to drown others in blood, as a warning against any attempt to change the structures of this system, to replace the free with the unfree, the just with the unjust, the good with the bad, the holy with the unholy, or the insane.

----

77. Could it be that he'd hoped his angry outburst would have the desired effect? That his son would bow to his father's wrath? He may have had a small (but intense) wish for this to happen. But in that case, it was a big gamble. Much too big a gamble. And if he had truly wished for this sort of desired effect: an irresponsibly big gamble.

----

78. Why, why? Did he realize what he was doing? Yes, he couldn't deny it. He couldn't deny it, because that would mean discounting what had happened. The father played a role in his son's decision to become an elite Norwegian soldier. The father had not prevented this; on the contrary, he had actually given

the situation a good shove. Without hesitating, you could say in cold blood, he had deliberately allowed his distress to govern his behavior such that his son couldn't avoid making the fatal decision, which, until now, he'd simply been toying with in his mind. Of course he was distressed, even unnerved, he thought it was terrible that his son would enlist as an elite soldier, even as he was about to complete what was, from Armand's point of view, a completely unnecessary compulsory military service; he wasn't merely pretending to be upset, the scorn he heaped on his son was no pretense, he meant it, deeply and sincerely, and he couldn't have controlled himself even if he'd wanted to. He took a chance. He allowed his own true state of mind to govern the whole situation, in cold blood.

———

79. He sacrificed his son. He knew he had sacrificed him. He wasn't happy about it. He was horrified. At himself. With open eyes he had allowed himself to lose his temper and thereby sacrificed his son. To war. To the most extreme of consequences. To the most secret and extreme of consequences, which cannot be concealed but takes place beyond words and for that reason is concealed. During the time when Armand V. was walking around in Oslo, waiting to be appointed ambassador to London or Paris, his crowning achievement, he sacrificed his son to war. An abyss. He knew why he did it, there was something inescapable about it, he could do nothing else.

———

80. On his regular monthly visit to the apartment building where his son rented a room from an old widow, whom

Armand had discovered, to his surprise, was malicious, he walked as usual up Kirkeveien from the Majorstua intersection, on the right-hand side, all the way until he came to Suhms Gate, which was part of the route previously mentioned as a detour to his son's place. The only thing irregular about Armand's walk this time was that it was happening early in the evening on a Friday, because it was now a month since his son had completed his compulsory military service and had immediately enlisted as a soldier in the elite force that was preparing for operations outside the country's borders, and Armand hoped that he'd now come to Oslo on leave and might show up at his room at about this time. He walked along Suhms Gate; the summer was waning, as evident in the fact that an early twilight was smoldering right behind, or in the shadow of, the clear air. Suddenly he heard hasty footsteps behind him, and a figure appeared at his side and began keeping pace with him as he walked. It was the young student who rented the other room from the old widow, and he explained that he was now on his way home after a long day at the university. Armand politely asked what he was studying, and then whether he'd seen anything of his son, his fellow lodger. The student had not, but on the other hand they'd never had much to do with each other; for that matter, the other lodger, his son, could have spent days in his room without the other renter, the student, even noticing. Especially if they had different schedules, the student added. By now they'd entered the neighborhood of the building where the old widow had a big apartment, and they were soon standing at the front entrance. Armand was about to ring the doorbell, using the one long signal they had agreed upon, but the young student stopped him, took out a key ring, and let them both in. They went upstairs, and in front of the door to the apartment the young student again took out his key ring to let them in. With a sweep of his arm he invited Armand to enter, but Armand replied, also with a gesture, by pointing to the doorbell and shaking his head at the student's invitation to cross the threshold. The young student understood then that Armand wanted to ring the bell so the old widow would personally have to let him in, so he nodded, stepped inside the apartment's hallway, and closed the door behind him. Then Armand rang the bell: one long signal. He waited. Eventually, he heard a rustling in the hallway, and a moment later the old widow opened the door a crack and stood there with her head tilted to one side. She stared at him through the crack in the door, and when she saw that it was Armand V., she opened the door a little more and let him in. She asked how he'd managed to get in the front entrance downstairs. Armand explained, but she made no comment. They went into the kitchen, where Armand opened his briefcase and took out the money and the rental book. She accepted the payment and signed the book, which she then returned to him. Armand put it back in his briefcase, closing it up. The widow put the money in what looked like a pocket of her clothing. Armand stared at the closed door to his son's room. The widow saw that he was staring at the closed door to his son's room, but she made no comment. Her malice was founded on bitterness. An inconceivable bitterness. Armand had tried to loosen things up somewhat by employing his diplomatic charm, but he had failed. Now he stood up to leave. His task was completed. But at that moment his son showed up, wearing his elite uniform, straight from the training center of the special battalion somewhere in central Norway. The son could see by his father's briefcase that he was here to pay the rent, and he was clearly not pleased about it. He'd planned to pay his own rent, he was making a good salary now, he said, and it was totally unnecessary for his father to pay for his room. But his father insisted on continuing to pay for the room. After that the son went back into his room to change into civilian clothes. The old widow now disappeared, retreating to the comfort of her inner sanctum. When the son had changed into civilian clothes, he opened the door to his room and asked if his father wanted to come in for a moment. Armand did so, sitting down on the straight-backed chair, while his son sat on the edge of the bed, dressed in civilian clothes. His father asked if he might invite him out to dinner that evening, but the son said that didn't suit him. But maybe on Sunday, Sunday afternoon, before he went back to his battalion and the strenuous but interesting training program he was undergoing in order to become an elite soldier. So that was what they agreed. After that the father stayed for a little longer. The son told him more about his initial experiences as an elite soldier. About what his days were like, about the training, about the camaraderie among the soldiers, in short, about his life in general, and once he began describing things, the words practically spilled out of him.

———

81. On Sunday, Armand met his son for dinner at a restaurant in central Oslo. It was Theatercaféen, across the street from the National Theater. They had agreed to meet at five o'clock, which

is the traditional hour for having dinner in Norway, including formal Sunday dinners. Even though the son had to return to the Special Forces training camp right after dinner, he showed up in civilian clothes. They ate a traditional Sunday dinner, with cauliflower soup, steak, and caramel pudding for dessert. They also shared a bottle of good red wine, which was pretty much empty by the time they finished the main course, so Armand asked the waiter for two glasses of a dessert wine that would go well with the pudding. Finally, they had coffee and a glass of liqueur. On Sundays Theatercaféen has a special atmosphere. On weekdays it is a buzzing café, filled with wealthy business-men and successful people from the film industry and advertis-ing agencies, as well as the occasional diplomat, but on Sunday it becomes a quiet place. On that day the café closes early (10 p.m.), and until that time it's frequented by people, both male and female, who don't usually eat out very often but who want to enjoy a Sunday dinner in a restaurant with their family or good friends. The prices are also much reduced for the Sunday menu, which was something that suited Armand, now that he'd invited his gluttonous son to dinner. It's true, he ate like a horse and Armand asked whether he'd like to order another steak, but his son declined with a smile. After dinner they sat for a short time enjoying their coffee and liqueur as they calmly and quietly conversed. But the son had to leave early, so Armand called for the waiter and asked for the check, which he paid with his credit card. They parted outside Theatercaféen. The son headed back to his room to change into his military uniform, and the father went home to spend Sunday evening thinking about life in gen-eral, and about his own life in particular. He felt that, in spite everything, something had happened at this dinner, something that might have to do with small, epic shifts.

––––––––––

82. About a month later, he went to the widow's apartment to pay his son's rent. It was once again a Friday, and he showed up at the same hour as last time. She accepted the money without giving any sign whatsoever that it meant anything to her, it was merely something regrettable but necessary, a ritual that she carried out to the letter with regard to the payment account book, signature and all. Lately he'd become curious about how her private inner sanctum might look, but this was something he never saw. She received him either at the telephone table in the long entry hall or in the kitchen, as she was doing now. He knew that he could have had a look at her other rooms if he'd gone into them, but in spite of his curiosity, he refrained from any tactics which he was certain would lead him to gain access to those rooms, possibly out of sheer indifference, when it came right down to it. (But he did ask his son whether he'd ever been in there, because if he had, he'd like his son to describe what he saw.) He paid the rent, glanced at his watch, and was about to leave. At that moment his son let himself into the apartment and, like a breath of fresh air, came down the long hallway, wearing his new uniform. He greeted his father and invited him to come into his room. There he sat down on the edge of the bed, while his father sat on a straight-backed chair. The father asked how he'd been since the last time they'd seen each other, and the son began telling him, apparently glad to be asked. But while he was talking, the door slowly opened and the

other renter, the student, quietly entered, almost indiscernibly closing the door behind him; with a look of agitation, he stood in front of Armand's son and said: "It's all over for me." Then he started to cry. Armand's uniformed son threw out his hands in bewilderment, then looked at his father. The student muttered: "Sorry" and again opened the door with a vague expression and disappeared, closing the door carefully after him. Armand felt uncomfortable and soon said goodbye to his son, even though his son clearly would have liked him to stay a little longer.

----

83. Of course I could have delved into the novel above and written it down. It would have taken a lot of work to lay it out, and in the end it would have been composed just as it was from the very beginning. Can I say that? Then what about the fact that all my novels have turned out differently than I thought they would when I first set out? In other words, a novel comes together little by little, but does that contradict the fact that it has been there all along, from the beginning? Hidden. Slumbering. Buried. No matter how much I repudiate the notion that the novel has been there from the beginning, I can't escape the possibility, at any rate, that it might be true after all. In fact, the more I contradict myself, the more convinced I am that I'm not contradicting myself, but that writing a novel means not inventing it, but uncovering it.

83 B. The original novel is about the Norwegian diplomat Armand V. I don't intend to write it down, but I'm making use of it in order to write the footnotes. Yet at times I may write

about characters in these footnotes who aren't found anywhere in the original novel; but of course this doesn't mean that these characters are any less fictional than those in the actual unwritten novel. The twin sister is one such character. She's the twin sister of N, Armand V.'s first wife, who is mentioned a great deal in the novel and who appears occasionally in these footnotes. Thus the twin sister has a unique place in this text presented here, because she doesn't belong to the premises for the footnotes, but is seen exclusively in relation to the material that has actually been written down. That makes her rare. Pay attention to her and treat her with as much vigilance as the author has devoted to her. The twin sister.

83 C. What is written here is not what happens in the original novel; these are footnotes to what has happened in there. Ongoing but perhaps coincidental, footnotes, which undoubtedly distort the original novel. So it would be most precise to say that these blocks of text, now presented, consist of ongoing but distorted footnotes to an unwritten novel.

83 D. A refusal. Why do I refuse to write the novel about Armand V.? Because it wouldn't work as a novel? How can I know that when I haven't tried to write it down? One thing is certain, however: wishing to write a novel about the Norwegian diplomat Armand V., I've decided the best way to realize this is not by writing a novel about him, but by allowing him instead to appear in an outpouring of footnotes to this novel. The sum of these footnotes, therefore, is the novel about Armand V. Linked to these footnotes are also the author's comments about what

he's doing, something that is also linked to the sum of these footnotes, which, taken as a whole, constitute the novel about Armand V. I'm now in the process of writing a series of these footnotes, and for the second time. That's why I call them footnotes about the relationship between the unwritten novel and the footnotes to this novel. Second section.

83 E. It all began in Venice. A Somali was outside the Londra Palace hotel. It was late in the evening, and the Somali was packing up his wares—handbags—which is what all the Somalis in Venice sold, this man outside the Londra Palace included. I was staying at the Londra Palace, and all day long I'd noticed this Somali. Now I was standing in the open window of my hotel room, staring down at the plaza that faced the Lagoon where the Somali was packing up his handbags. He had been standing in the same spot all day, and I wondered how much he managed to rake in over the course of a day, and how much he would eventually be allowed to keep. Suddenly he turned his head, glanced up at my hotel window, and saw me. He might have noticed that I'd been watching him, and he now stood there, craning his neck and staring up at me. He started to laugh. His laughing tongue was bright red. And I stood there. In the window of my room in the Londra Palace, observed by the man whom I'd been observing. The laughing Somali down there, and me up above in the open window of the Londra Palace hotel. He didn't seem threatening, he was a laughing Somali in Venice, a survivor, who was laughing at the man in the window of the Londra Palace hotel. Yet there was something threatening about us, and there and then I had an idea for a novel, in a

single flash. My novel. Impossible, I thought. It's impossible, and I know it, and now I have to suffer the consequences of what I've known for a long time. From now on I will write only footnotes. Although this insight, from a human point of view, was extremely disheartening, from an artistic point of view it was an edifying thought.

I was unable to explain, even to myself in some wordless language, what a brilliant idea for a novel this was, other than the conviction that from now on I had to write footnotes. But I immediately coupled it to Thomas Mann and Joseph Brodsky and understood it to mean that in some way or other, I was to write footnotes to Brodsky's *Watermark* or Thomas Mann's *Death in Venice*. A strange coupling, between third-world problems and an ambitious literary project that was totally separate from the former.

83 F.   On closer examination, I've come to the realization that what the previous footnote says is wrong. Meaning I've remembered things wrong. When I arrived in Venice—this was in June 2004—I had already decided to work with footnotes. In fact, I'd already decided to make footnotes to Joseph Brodsky's *Watermark* when I suddenly got an idea for a novel and a Somali handbag vendor—whom I'd been watching, both down below in the plaza in front of the Lagoon and from my hotel window—turned toward my hotel window late in the evening, craned his neck and observed me as I stood there smoking a cigarette. Then he began to laugh at me, with his bright red tongue. *This* idea for a novel meant that I lost sight of the footnote idea, replaced by this new idea that was born at that precise moment.

This idea soon faded. It didn't survive the night; by the following morning it was gone—both the subject matter which, by the way, had never been clear since it consisted of a flash of insight, and also the very fact that I'd even had the idea. I didn't remember it until now, as I'm writing this. But I hadn't forgotten the idea about the footnotes for *Watermark*, and in September of that year I decided to make it happen.

I mention all this—Venice, the sinking city, my room at the Londra Palace (with its window facing the plaza in front of the Lagoon), the Somali, and myself, at the moment when, in a flash, I had a brilliant, unknown idea for a novel, which must have been about my affiliation with the imperialistic system, and the fact that in my memory I've combined all of this with what I wanted to write in a work based on footnotes (originally footnotes to another author's work, but later footnotes to an unknown and unwritten but possibly writable novel by me)—I mention it because I think that all of this, including the distortion of memory, has significance for everything that I have attempted here to say.

83 G. I have only one life to live. And I am the one writing this.

83 H. Let's get straight to the point. Why am I doing it this way? Why am I avoiding writing the novel about Armand, as it exists, embryonic, in my consciousness, the way I've always written all my other novels, allowing the words to emerge and spill out? I know I've said that I want to do something completely different. Can that be it? Something completely different from before, now that I have very few novels left to write?

831. I'm writing on overtime. My literary output ended with *T. Singer*, written and published in 1999. Everything after that is an exception, which will never be repeated. Including this.

83J. When I now resist delving into the unwritten novel the way I've always delved into it and drawn it forward, it's because I'm afraid of doing so. I'm afraid of what might result from such work. My time is past, I can accept that. I cannot delve into the unwritten novel and draw it forward, only to see that the result doesn't hold up. That it isn't up to my standard. I don't think the result would have been weak. Just a little weaker than what is my usual standard. And I don't want that. It's not my style.

83K. Way in the back of my mind is an absurd notion that I have a responsibility toward humankind. (Is that the same thing as being responsible for humankind? I don't think so.) I can present a good argument as to why I don't have this sort of responsibility, nor do I think anyone would seriously point out to me that I have such a responsibility. But there it is.

And sometimes I fall to my knees (in my mind) to say thank you for this unreasonable notion that I have about myself.

_____

84. Even here "the novel" doesn't give me anything close to the meaning you would expect it to give. I'm not sure if that's because the novel is invisible. Or because it can only be glimpsed, now and then. You have to accept the consequences of what is unclear, merely glimpsed, even what is indifferent about this

novel. This lack of coherence is extremely troublesome, yet at the same time extremely accurate with regard to the way life is experienced by someone like me. As far as I know, the story has now taken a turn away from what I previously meant to be its central focus: that it's some sort of story about Everyman. Now that's no longer true, and at this point Armand has passed sixty-five, he has passed the time of the first footnote. Is now the time to talk about the Disappointment? Disappointment about the fact that you're no longer living in your own time, but in someone else's era? Which of course seems noisy. So: the Disappointment and the noise. The words of an aging man. An aging man cursing the future and its men (and women). The sound and the fury. The unbearable noise and the bitter disappointment. The time to ask for communication is apparently over. If this could coincide with an understanding of the invisible novel, with which I've been fumbling for more than a year now, I would not be unhappy. Everything that falls into place is lovely to behold, even if it precludes your own inclusion.

---

85. There comes a time when you step away from the ranks of your family, though you're still alive. That's when you've become shadow. Some people become shadow too early, others much too late. Armand feared that he became shadow much too late; in fact, that he hadn't yet become that. Armand's situation was perhaps the worst. In three weeks he was going to meet the Twin Sister, up in the mountains. He knew he had to appear before her as Shadow. It was a question of keeping his part of the agreement that had been made long ago.

85B. P.S. There's a difference between being a shadow, or Shadow, and finding yourself in the shadow, living a shadowy life, and so on. As a reader, and human being, you should not confuse these things. Or else you'll lose your sense of direction.

----

86. Love of luxury. Vanity. Clothing. Sparkling wines. Life in all its incomparableness. I can't help the fact that I'm going to miss it, thought Armand. I'm totally dependent on it. This is what everything in me has striven toward, and I've achieved it. You.

"Me?"

"Yes, you."

"Thanks," she said.

"For what?"

"For describing life in all its incomparableness. I'm an old gray-haired but beautiful woman from the upper class in a little town in Vestland, close to the Atlantic Ocean."

"I've been there."

"I know. I was there back then too, at home, with you."

----

87. This book will remain in chaos until New Year's. After that I'll write it down in its final version. See, by the way, footnotes 83A-K (about the fact that the finished novel exists beforehand and merely has to be written down, along with all sorts of possible dead ends and almost-attempts, which are due to our inadequacy).

88. Armand's dream. The darkness of the theater is filled with expectant spectators as Armand steps onto the illuminated stage. He is strangely excited about this meeting with his audience, and he's looking forward to launching into his eternal monologue. But suddenly he discovers that he's a fox. He is looking at himself from the outside and sees that he has a fox face, a fox body, and a thick fox tail. This terrifies him, and he looks for a means of escape. Then he notices the twin sister sitting on the stage, ready to sing. Armand throws himself at her, hiding his head in her arms. Now nobody will see that I'm a fox, he thinks.

89. This book will remain in chaos until New Year's. After that I'll write it down in its final version. But everything depends on the sacrifice of the son. God = U.S.A. God = U.S.A. That means that Armand accepts the dominance of the U.S.A. (And hasn't he actually already done that in my footnotes?)

90. Somewhere or other, at a military airstrip in Norway, in the eastern region, two military planes take off, on their way toward a mission. Two big war planes. In my consciousness there are two planes, not one. Two big war planes.

91. Finally, the last appointment. The trip to London. Moving into the residence in one of London's prestigious neighbor-

hoods, an embassy residence highly regarded among the corps diplomatique in this cosmopolitan city. The moving van: a big semitruck. The workers unload the heavy, privately owned furniture and carry everything inside the residence. As in a movie. A more detailed description of the residence will have to wait, the same holds true for a description of the private quarters. A big day. But it can't be concealed that the person writing this is more naively enthusiastic than the one he's writing about, who is now going to live here.

––––––––––

92. On his way to the Palace. Taken by carriage. The horses. Through the narrow streets to Buckingham Palace. Up the wide staircase. Huge doors are thrown open by guards. He waits. Then, inside for the audience. Delivering his credentials from His Majesty the King of Norway. Her Majesty the Queen of England accepts them. All of this Armand experienced with no sense of irony. He was participating in a game. He felt the ritual's gravity. He was vain down to his fingertips because he was the one who had the great honor of playing a role in this drama. He felt like an important fool in a vast historic machinery. Afterward, he refused to talk about it.

––––––––––

93. While Armand was getting settled in London, his son returned home. Still in uniform. This time the father didn't see the son's return because he was in London, but that didn't matter because the son didn't see anything either. He was blind. A blind soldier returned home. To Norway. To Oslo. To the big hospital that could not effect a cure.

94. As soon as the father heard what had happened, he went to Oslo. He went to see his son at the hospital, sitting down on the edge of his son's bed in the private room. For the first time in many years he also met his son's mother, to whom he was married many years ago. He had a long talk with the specialist who was treating his son. After a month he returned to London. Together with his son. The father went to get his son in Oslo and brought him to London, where he was the Norwegian ambassador. The son was sent to the best doctors this cosmopolitan city could offer, and it turned out nothing could be done. But before that became clear, the father devoted himself to getting his son the best training in how to read Braille. Time passed. The son acquired a white cane, which he used to make his way around the residence of the Norwegian embassy in London. He made progress at reading Braille. The father tried to help his young son keep up his courage. He constantly pointed out that it was necessary for his son to show strength of will and not allow himself to be completely trapped by the discouraging knowledge that he was blind and would be for the rest of his life.

95. In the month of July, the son flew alone to Oslo in order to vacation with his mother in Norway. A couple of weeks later Armand also flew to Norway and took his son for a weeklong stay in the mountains. They booked rooms in the B and B run by the twin sister. The father introduced the twin sister as "the mother" of the son's half sister, the one whose father was Armand. They went on very short mountain hikes that nevertheless

took a long time, because the son didn't yet feel confident about navigating the mountainous terrain now that he could no longer see. His white cane gleamed as he, along with his spry and gray-haired father, stumbled his way forward. His father spoke quietly about the ever-shifting clouds in the sky and about what the relationship was like between the blue sky and the cloud formations at any specific time. He, meaning Armand, noticed that the color yellow kept reappearing, both when he described the sky and when he described nature in general. He'd never noticed this before, that the yellowness of nature played such a big role, both in the sky and on the mountain slopes; it wasn't the dominant color, but there was still a remarkable dynamism about the yellow, almost hidden as it often was, behind a gray veil in the sky. In addition to describing their surroundings, he also frequently challenged his son to feel the wind gusting toward them.

And as the rain began to fall from the now black sky, striking them as big, clear, individual drops, he said: "Feel that? It's starting to rain, so we need to turn around."

And they would head back to the twin sister's B and B, and they were often soaking wet before they got there, even though it wasn't far away, but the son couldn't walk very fast. Other times they would both notice that rain was coming their way because they heard thunder. Then Armand would propose they should keep walking, because it could be a while before the thunderstorm was overhead. So they continued on until they reached a high-plateau landscape, surrounded on all sides by towering slopes that got blacker and more intense in color as the thunder got closer.

"I think we'll turn around," said Armand. "Hear that? The thunder is right above the nearest ridge."

At that moment lightning flashed. The air was split open by wild lightning, again that yellowness of Armand's description, but it was now a completely different kind of yellow, more glaring. A lightning bolt struck only sixty or seventy meters from where they were standing. Armand was just about to exclaim: "Did you see that! Did you see that!" but he managed to restrain himself. The worst thing was that he was convinced his son had, in fact, seen it, even though he was blind. Then it started to rain. Even though they found themselves in a desolate landscape, apparently closed in by mountains on all sides, Armand knew that they were only a few hundred meters from the twin sister's B and B, and he began leading his son in that direction. Soaking wet, they arrived at the B and B where they dried off and changed every stitch of clothing they had on. After that, they ate lunch in the dining room. There were other guests, but they were able to get a table all to themselves, as they usually did. After lunch the weather cleared, as Armand lay on his bed and relaxed in his room. He got up and threw open the window. How wonderfully clean the air was outside! He left his room and went across the hall to knock on his son's door, and when his son answered, he went in. He said the weather was now glorious and all of nature had been cleansed by the morning storm, so he suggested they spend the afternoon going on a long hike. By "long" he meant of course lengthy in terms of time, not distance. But his son didn't want to do that. He said he was tired, he didn't have the energy. Armand knew that his son had good reason to feel worn out, maybe even disheartened.

Getting dressed and undressed had now become an unfamiliar and strenuous task for him; having to shed soaking wet clothes had proved especially disheartening, a feeling that only time would heal. But Armand refused to give in, he used his obvious powers of persuasion, and finally the son relented. He grabbed his white cane and followed his father downstairs to the lobby and then outside into the fresh air. They took a different hiking trail this time, heading up a slope, and suddenly they heard the jangling of rusty bells. It was a flock of goats on the scree, and the animals had now noticed them and approached.

"Sheep," said the son, quite pleased.

Armand said nothing, but when the goats came so close that it was possible to touch them, he took his son's hand, put it on the goat's shaggy coat, and said: "Feel that, feel that!"

The son kept his hand on the goat's shaggy coat for a while, touching and sniffing (breathing in the cleansed air), and then he said: "Goats. They're goats." At that the startled goat bounded away from him, followed by the whole flock. But they stopped to regroup a short distance away, and a few minutes later once again approached. Armand and his son walked slowly through the flock of goats, listening to the rusty bells on the lead goat, the scree glittering with raspberries, and they continued upward, along a narrow trail, and the son used his cane to feel his way forward, the whole time encouraged by his old father, who offered comments, speaking in a serious and matter-of-fact tone of voice. After a while they agreed to turn around and go back to the B and B to rest before dinner was served at seven. It had been a long day, invigorating in a way, but also strenuous, just as every day would be from now on, all of them continuing to be strenuous and taxing.

96. *The argumentation.*

In London as the Norwegian ambassador, with his blind son, the young disabled soldier. They were now back after their stay in the Norwegian mountains during the summer. Armand had to make certain he didn't turn against those who had instigated this war which had made his son into a disabled veteran. His own country was a participant in this war, and as a diplomat he had acted fully within the appropriate parameters and in accordance with the prevailing views. The fact that he considered the war unwise, even rash, was another story which never, even for a moment, affected the views he represented. It's true that he had allowed himself a few, shall we say ironic, remarks about the war, but they were so disguised that hardly anyone else understood the irony in his words; he had also been able, in the strictest privacy, when he was alone in his own bedroom in the residence of the magnificent Norwegian embassy in South Kensington, London, after a long day, to cast aside his official attire and allow himself to sink into a much longed-for and malicious merriment at the impossible world he lived in, as an obedient servant to those in power, both willingly and unwillingly; *willingly* because with open eyes he had voluntarily entered the diplomatic corps in his younger days, and *unwillingly* because the small country whose diplomatic corps he had joined acted as an obedient servant to the major world power, which was something he—by the way and of course—had been fully aware of when he joined the Norwegian foreign service. Yet this stopped when he received word about what had happened to his son.

It came as a shock to him. Even though he knew that his son was on a secret military mission, he hadn't ceased his biting and sarcastic comments in the presence of others with regard to that very war, something about which he laughed long and hard whenever he was alone in his own bedroom, freed from his official attire. Naturally it had crossed his mind that something might happen to his son, but he had dismissed the idea as highly unlikely, since he had told himself that of course a father, from a psychological point of view, has reason to worry about a son who is on a military mission in the Far East; but he shouldn't forget that statistically it was no more dangerous to be in uniform and armed to the teeth, serving with a superior Western military power in impoverished Asia, than it was to be in civilian clothes behind the wheel of a car, exposed to a potentially slippery fate on one of the countless highways that lead into London, for example. So he had dismissed the idea that his son might be in great danger in this war, which he personally opposed, yet which he, as a diplomatic official, had to support. Then word came about his son's abrupt return home from the Asian mountain plateau. A young man without sight. Blind forevermore. And since then he had been focused on his son's future.

Armand did all he could to make sure his son would be able to endure his fate. He had brought him to London and the ambassador's residence because of the proximity to the city of a highly respected institute or school for the blind, and he'd managed to get his son accepted there, not simply because he was an ambassador, but also because the cause of his son's blindness had opened all doors, both official and unofficial. That was where his son now spent the weekdays, busily occupied with trying, if at all possible, to make his ruined sight into less of an over- whelming tragedy. There he learned to see with his fingers, with his sense of smell, with his ears, with his mouth, his skin, even with his shoulder blades, and thereby also to see what those with sight couldn't see, meaning what existed and moved on the other side, away from the direction in which the eyes always looked. On weekends the son went to stay with his father in his residence. In the beginning Armand would pick him up in one of the embassy cars, sitting in the driver's seat himself, but the goal was for his son eventually to take the train on his own, so his father could meet him at the station in London.

Most of the time during these weekend visits in London the son would stay indoors, inside the residence, except for a short walk in a public park, either on Saturday or Sunday morning, as suggested by his father. Armand also liked to take him to concerts and the theater. Concerts as a respite, and the theater so that he could learn to bear his fate, because even though he would never see again, he could still, if he used all the other senses in his possession, experience the atmosphere inside the theater, and maybe even, at moments, find joy. Armand also hoped that in the big, glorious theater halls his son might be inspired to throw himself into practicing his new skills, which were now utterly vital to his life. Listening to the silence in the hall during the performance, the intense listening and atten- tiveness of the audience, the words spoken on stage, which he could apprehend just as well as anyone else even though he couldn't actually see the stage set and props, or the lighting, etc., but he could capture all of this in other ways, if need be by having his companion, Armand, whisper to him what *he* was able to see on the stage.

One play they went to see was *Brand* by Henrik Ibsen. By virtue of his position as the Norwegian ambassador, Armand had been invited to the premiere at the National Theatre, and his son went with him, taking along his white cane. During the performance they both paid close attention; the son because he found it amusing to listen to this play, which he knew in his own language, now being performed in English, with English rhyme schemes, and Armand because he had a certain relationship to this particular play and was wondering how this excellent cast would manage to relate to what Armand called the *Brand*-folly of our time. After the performance they were invited to a reception backstage, where they said hello to the theater management and actors, and where Armand used the occasion to offer a toast, such as was appropriate for Norway's ambassador in London, one that was brief, to the point, and dryly witty, since he knew this was what the Brits would appreciate.

Armand was carrying out his duties. Even though he'd suffered a personal tragedy within his immediate family, it did not strip him of his ability to act as the Norwegian ambassador in London. He did not turn against those who had instigated this war from which his son had returned a disabled veteran. If he felt a deep rage toward the United States, he never expressed it. If he had, the result would have been that he would be honorably discharged from his position as the Norwegian envoy, and he would have then entered the ranks of retirees. It would have been no more than a mild and tactful reaction on his part, if the rage at those who had involved us in this war, which had ruined his son's life, had been allowed to surge in his breast. And subsequently led to this tactful breach on his part. Quiet but irrevocable. And if he'd actually accessed the depths of his rage, then he would have proclaimed to his Norwegian employer, for whom he'd spent the past forty years working, the true nature of his blistering protest, which would make it necessary for him to leave the foreign service immediately, and he wouldn't hesitate to make his reason public in a letter to the editor sent to one of his country's biggest daily newspapers. But none of this happened. Truth be told, he never even considered such a possibility. Not even the first possibility of the tactful but decisive breach. Armand had apparently not accessed the depths of his rage. Why not? Could it be because that sort of deep rage did not exist inside him, that there was no snarling beast in there that wished to free itself from its human (civilized) chains?

Armand continued in his official position. There was nothing astonishing about that. On the contrary, anything else would have been astonishing. If Armand had possessed a deep rage inside him, and if he had accessed this uncivilized beast way down inside, at the very bottom, he still couldn't have behaved differently than he did. Most likely such a deep rage did exist, but it was of no use, and if Armand had been confronted by this claim, he would have, again most likely, nodded agreement, and added: And that's a good thing. Armand continued in his official position. He cursed no one. It was of no use. And that was a good thing. Armand carried on as he had before. He was nearing the end of his career, which he was finishing up in the sought-after position as the Norwegian ambassador in London. An incomprehensible tragedy, however, had resulted in him being constantly, both visibly and invisibly, accompanied by a young man with a white cane as he carried out his duties. Enabling his son to bear his fate was something that was always on his mind, both day and night. Every Sunday evening he would drive his son back to the first-class institute that would help him prepare for his new life, which was now based on greatly limited conditions, and he would say goodbye on the steps leading to the pleasant reception area, which his son preferred to enter alone. What was Armand thinking about after he delivered his son to the institute and drove back to London late on a Sunday evening, sitting comfortably on the leather seat behind the wheel and the technically advanced dashboard in his steel-reinforced embassy car, which, seen from the outside, was merely two bright head-lights among all the other dual sets of lights moving forward in a long line toward the metropolis on that evening? This and the following are an attempt to explain. It has to do with Armand's lengthy series of arguments, which he, point by point, could not avoid pursuing on his journey toward the inevitable, something about which he'd always known, yet had never intended to pursue. Such that when all this is combined, put together, it will end with the inevitable, which cannot be pursued.

When it first occurred to Armand, back when he was in his late twenties, that he actually could choose a career with the diplomatic corps, he hadn't hesitated to make the decision. If his life had progressed differently—without this unfortunate yearning in his youth for glamour (even glitz and glitter) and comfort and with the whole world as his stage, which he thought stood gloriously open to him when he realized that he could actually become a diplomat—if he had instead settled for a meager life and the possibility of making an academic career for himself, then he wasn't certain, not even now, that he would have valued it very highly. No, he would have made the exact same choice now, as an aging gentleman, as he had with youth's boundless craving for a global life experienced in the reflection of vanity. Added to this was a third aspect that had been decisive in his assessments, which enhanced for him the attractiveness of the Norwegian foreign service: he was a player. He regarded himself as a player, and it was precisely this aspect about himself that Armand would not deny, even today, although he had to admit that the young Armand had overestimated both the fascination of the game and the opportunities available to him, something that had turned him into a fundamental cynic who did not acknowledge any deeper commitment to the duties he carried out for the powers he served. He hadn't felt the need to commit to what he said or did. He didn't need to stand behind his own words or deeds, as a means of assuring himself that he could carry out his obligations. This lent him a delightful feeling of independence. He hadn't needed to invest himself in his diplomatic advancements; he could effortlessly focus on his official career and ensure that his conduct was always formally satisfactory to those he had agreed to serve. He had only an outward loyalty to those he represented. His joy at inwardly being a cynic in the (small) Norwegian foreign service had been great, even exceptional. The extent to which he agreed, or did not agree, with the gestures, statements, and attitudes that he was obligated to employ at all times, was basically quite irrelevant to him. And by the way, this was also irrelevant to his colleagues within the foreign service. His cynicism was well known—and accepted, even though Armand thought that his sense of irony, for the most part, was not understood by anyone other than himself. And that might well be true, when it came to those things that were closest to his heart, but there's no doubt that most people within the Norwegian foreign service were well aware of his cynical nature, which they often discussed among themselves as Armand V.'s unsentimental way of getting hold of things, and which Armand himself considered his great strength as a diplomat. Just think of all the sentimentality I've avoided, not having to lay it on thick in all the contexts in which I've found myself; just think of how I could have been in the vanguard of sprinkling all sorts of intimacies around the Norwegian diplomatic corps, intimacies that would have made it completely impossible to function with all that tender-heartedness and naïveté in a cynical world, he thought. They really ought to have thanked me, because I've always kept a clear head and restricted all my emotions to my private quarters, he thought. And basically that's what he'd done. The crowning achievement had been his reward. The much sought-after appointment as the Norwegian envoy to Great Britain, the ambassadorship in London. Yet it couldn't be denied that he had now become a victim of these very same powers that he had so loyally served in such a skeptical and disloyal way, he thought. How can I accept that without falling apart?

Armand V. in service to his little Norwegian nation. With its strong, even unflinching, tie to the world's mightiest nation, the United States. A population of less than five million people, but an economically strong nation. Favored with rich natural resources that could be exploited at times when there was particularly great interest in such resources in terms of international economic policies. During the Cold War, which had just ended, it had been a nation with a strategically central role, in terms of the military. Now, it was still an important oil-producing nation, with good statistical probability of oil-rich finds in unexplored Norwegian waters off the long coastline. An interesting country for its kindly disposed ally, the super-power United States, as well as for the European nations. For this small nation's distanced foreign service agent, currently the country's ambassador in London, it was a question of surviving under such circumstances without losing himself.

Because he did fear losing himself. In other words, he feared ceasing to relate to what was noble in his own life. In other words, he feared damnation. It had been there the whole time, as a threat, but now it had become acute. The fact that I can continue as before is a sign that I haven't lost myself, he thought. It has merely reinforced my fear of that happening, and that's good, even though it's more troublesome than ever before. In fact, it can seem like sheer hell, and I really have to pull myself together in order to find the energy to fulfill obligations—and joys, he thought as he pulled into the driveway to the residence in South Kensington. It was late on Sunday evening, and he used his key card and the coded panels to let himself into the magnificent building where a new week awaited his efforts, official signatures, and diplomatic judgment, often his insight as well, before he could again drive off in one of the embassy cars to pick up his son for another weekend in London.

Serve his God? Armand was an atheist, or rather an agnostic. Serve his country? Armand, in his heart, had been a disloyal servant to his country, although not outwardly. Serve his society? Armand feared he was a hanger-on, regardless of how that was viewed. Now he was going to pick up his son, whom he had not prevented from becoming a professional soldier in a special unit that had fought the war to which Armand himself was strongly opposed, and who had returned from that war disabled. Yet the claim is made here, once again, that if Armand cannot be connected with a noble life, then he quite simply does not exist.

The son often spent Friday evening, or Saturday evening, alone in his father's residence in London since Armand was frequently busy on the weekends, attending events that required Norway to be represented on the ambassador level. These events often had an aura of grandeur about them, taking place in the full radiance of crystal chandeliers, with livery-clad servants waiting on the guests, and Armand would attend wearing coat and tails. During one of these events—it must have been on a Saturday evening—he met the American ambassador. Actually, rather than say that he met the American ambassador, it would be more fitting to say that he ran into him. It was in the sparkling clean men's room, where they had both gone to relieve their bladders, and they stood side by side at the urinals, each attending to business as they chatted amiably with each other. At first Armand had been alone in the enormous, sparkling white men's room, and he'd found that a bit odd since there were so many people at this official event which he had been required to attend, and the fact that only one person, meaning himself, should find a need to take a piss at a specific moment seemed rather unlikely. But then he heard the door open, and in came another penguin, which was how many would describe, as Armand often did himself, the tuxedo-attired gentlemen, and the man came hurrying over to the urinal next to Armand instead of, as Armand would have done in his place, taking up position at one of the twenty available urinals farther away, and he immediately began chatting amiably with Armand about the sort of work they shared, getting right to the point as he unzipped his fly. It was the American ambassador. Armand had met him before, several times in fact, he'd even had lunch with him on two occasions, because the ways of diplomacy are inscrutable, and sometimes it may be that questions Washington wishes to have answered—for example sensitive questions regarding the Middle East—cannot always be put forth via a conversation between the United States ambassador in Damascus or Cairo and the Norwegian ambassador in those same cities, but instead can be discussed more appropriately, or at least be put forth more cautiously, at a lunch between Washington's representative in London and the Kingdom of Norway's representative in that same city, even though Norway actually has nothing whatsoever to do with those sensitive questions. So Armand knew him well, though it's not easy to say whether the American ambassador felt he knew Armand well, but perhaps it can be assumed he did. At any rate, the American ambassador chatted away, covering topics that extended from his fly to his tails, and from his tails to the soles of his feet. Armand was more reserved. He wished he could have made a joke about the man's head. The American's head. The American's head was disproportionate. To describe it fully you'd have to say that his head towered on top of his shoulders, not that it towered on top of his neck, which would be the usual thing to say. His neck, throat, and head formed a single unit, a massive, fleshy unit. His neck was huge, having expanded to vast proportions, most likely having grown in width throughout the ambassador's entire career, steadily and progressively, all the way around. On the front of what could be called the head there was a face that was incredibly fleshy, but equally pronounced and strong in character. Because the entire head consisted of the neck, throat, and face, he looked like a pig, because that's what is precisely so characteristic about a pig, the only difference being that the front of the pig's massive head is called the snout, while it was labeled the "face" when it came to the American ambassador. So the American ambassador had the head of a pig, and that made Armand act reserved as he stood there talking to the amiable man from Washington. They stood there urinating into the urinals. Armand hadn't noticed that the American ambassador had a pig's head on the previous occasions they'd met, though he should have noticed since it was so obvious, but of course that was because the circumstances of their previous meetings hadn't lent themselves to such observations. He, Armand, was after all a diplomat from a friendly nation vis-à-vis the American ambassador, and naturally there were certain limitations to the sort of observations he could allow himself to make, face-to-face, to the ambassador of the equally friendly world power, the United States. But this time they happened to meet by accident, and under such casual circumstances that Armand could allow himself to take a close look, and then he saw what he saw. He didn't like what he saw. He felt very uncomfortable. Especially because the American ambassador kept on chatting, as if his pig's head caused him no embarrassment whatsoever. But it was embarrassing for Armand V. He knew that when he was back at his residence late in the evening, he would hope that his son had gone to bed and wasn't pacing in the room that was his, using his white cane, so that he, Armand, could make his way unnoticed to his own bedroom, take off his official attire, and go straight to bed. He knew he would not reflect on what he'd experienced that evening, as was his habit, often with great and unrestrained, sometimes caustic glee. He knew he would be afraid to fall asleep because he was afraid the pig's head would haunt his dreams and remain there, but he knew that he would nevertheless force himself to go straight to bed and hope for the best, hoping that the pig's head would be gone when he woke up in the morning. In the meantime, he was here. Together with the envoy from Washington who happened to have a pig's head. They were standing next to each other, urinating into their separate urinals. Armand finished first and turned around to go over to the sink to wash his hands. He took his time and also rinsed his face. A moment later the American ambassador also finished urinating, and he came over to the sink. He stood at the sink right next to Armand, and when he saw that the Norwegian ambassador was washing his face, he did the same. The American ambassador washed his pig's head with a little, contented squeal. As he dried his face with a small towel, Armand watched the American ambassador also drying his face and hands while chatting amiably with his Norwegian friend, saying something confidential. Armand nodded as he tried to smile. Yes, he did try to smile, since he was, after all, an experienced diplomat. They headed for the exit. The man with the pig's head held open the door for Armand to allow him to go first. But Armand didn't want to do that. He motioned for the American ambassador to exit first, to be followed by Armand V. from Norway. But the American ambassador insisted. He gave a pleased wink with his pig's head and insisted. He seemed greatly pleased with himself. But Armand repeated his courteous gesture and said: "Youth before beauty." That's when the whole scene changed. The American ambassador's expression changed completely. He gave Armand a nasty look. His pig's snout turned malicious, frightening. His body went rigid with rage. He waved his hand resolutely as he glared at Armand and then at the door. Armand obeyed. He could tell there was no other option. This was no joke, and Armand walked past the American ambassador who stood there with a furious expression on his pig's head as he deigned to allow Armand to go past.

Armand, wearing his coat and tails, walked up the stairs and into the glittering ceremonial halls, one after the other. Since he felt a strong need to compose himself, he found a door that led out onto a terrace facing an illuminated English park. He stood on the terrace, next to a pillar, and lit a cigarette, which he smoked, and in that manner finished an endlessly long series of arguments. He decided that he might as well do it now, there was no reason to postpone it any further. He'd seen enough, experienced enough, understood enough. For an aging gentleman who was also a diplomat, in fact the Norwegian ambassador to Great Britain, there's nothing new under the sun; even discovering that the American ambassador has a pig's head shouldn't be cause for either surprise or alarm. Especially not for him, Armand V. He was not alarmed. About what he'd seen.

About the fact that he'd seen it. About the fact that he hadn't avoided seeing it, but had actually acknowledged that he'd seen it and then behaved in accordance with this sight that was at first embarrassing and then gruesome. And so real, so true to nature. But weren't there other ways to describe the American ambassador? Such as a face that was resolute and strong in character, or maybe a somewhat roughly chiseled and massive face that nevertheless redeems itself upon closer acquaintance. That was how he could imagine ambassadors from other friendly nations might write home to their governments in secret reports after being asked to describe their impressions of the new American ambassador in London. Why couldn't he have seen the American ambassador in the same way when the ambassador came over and stood next to him at the urinals? Instead of being embarrassed by the fact that the Washington envoy had a pig's head, why couldn't he have thought of it as a face that was "resolute and strong in character," that might even seem appealing "upon closer acquaintance?" Then it would also have been easier to live with the American ambassador's display of power. Of course I can turn around and go back into the ceremonial hall, thought Armand, go back into the splendidly lit hall and casually stroll around until I catch sight of the American ambassador again, from a certain distance, so that he doesn't catch sight of me, and from a distance I could observe him and find out that I'm wrong about him having a pig's head; no one is treating him conspicuously, everyone is showing him the proper respect as he stands there, a somewhat chunky man, though for an American you might say he's merely powerfully built, and with a somewhat rough, but friendly and amiable face atop his powerful body. That's all I need to do, and then I'll be able to regain my peace of mind. It's true that I ended up in disfavor down there, but the person I fell into disfavor with is just an ordinary man, and not a bestial monster, and besides, it was a private matter, not a diplomatic situation. But Armand did not do this. It was pointless. Because there was no doubt that Armand had both seen and thought that this man who came into the men's room after Armand was already there and stood at the urinal next to him to relieve himself, had indeed possessed a pig's head that was so real, so true to nature. That was a fact, and Armand could not get around it. It does not go unpunished if you see that the American ambassador has a pig's head and then try not to see it. As do all the others in this hall, thought Armand.

But the power he displayed really scared me, Armand then thought. Why such uninhibited rage, and real willingness, an uninhibited willingness to express it over such a trivial matter? Because instead of modestly thanking the Washington envoy in London for being generous enough to allow me to exit the men's room first and even holding the door open for me, I failed to appreciate this generosity and responded as if I thought I could display the same generosity and hold the door open for him. That was stupid, but even worse was my remark. "Youth before beauty." What I meant to say, of course, was "youth before age," but I got confused. Maybe because it must have occurred to me that it would seem inappropriate to call him a "youth," since he looks to be, after all, a man in his late fifties, so almost a contemporary of mine, and for that reason I changed age to beauty, or rather, what I should have said was beauty before age, but that's equally stupid; no, it must have been his pig's head that made me uncomfortable. That must have been it, because what I, finally, came up with was that his so-called youth had to go before my own beauty, and that says everything about how he must have taken my view of what his beauty was, and he almost had reason to act as insulted as he did. And yet: the power he displayed scared me.

It was the power he displayed, without any cause, when it comes right down to it, that was frightening. Would it have seemed as frightening if Armand hadn't noticed that the American ambassador had a pig's head? If so, this episode wouldn't have taken place. The pig's head was the decisive element. It's not so easy for you to get rid of a pig's head, thought Armand pensively, and by "you" he meant the person he was addressing, which was himself. He knew he had encountered himself down there in the men's room. Here was the power under which he lived and whose servant he was. He had taken part in something primeval tonight. Raw power was displayed. Bestial. These were the primeval conditions under which Armand so stylishly lived. And which he was definitely unwilling to give up. At the same time, it's clear that a somewhat aging Norwegian gentleman who runs into the American ambassador in London in the men's room and discovers that the man has a pig's head is no longer capable of carrying out his diplomatic duties for his country. This was now Armand's big dilemma.

The dilemma consisted of the fact that he was incapable of leaving the diplomatic corps. Both because of a certain familiarity combined with outward prestige, and also because of other reasons, which will soon come to light. Quite simply, it was a matter of feeling at home, or belonging, if you will. Armand felt at home in this Western cultural circle, it was his culture. Regardless of how interested he might be in other countries, or how much he learned about them—their history, religion, etc.—and no matter how much he enjoyed finding out about their customs, even adopting these customs when appropriate, and with the greatest respect, there were and would always be those countries that required actual dialogue. When Armand thought he observed that the American ambassador in London had a pig's head, Armand was acting as an agent for others. That was not what he wanted, but the fact was that he was acting as an enemy agent when he saw such sights. Hence the horror he felt. For the others, those who were foreign, this was a normal sight. Considering the present state of the world, they would not be surprised that an American ambassador should appear with a pig's head when he issued his directives; that was why those who saw such sights were called "the others," the "evil" or the "hostile" ones, etc. Even ambassadors from so-called friendly regimes in the so-called third world weren't entirely uncomprehending about seeing such sights as Armand had seen in the men's room during that glittering event tonight. If Armand had said to the Egyptian ambassador, for instance: Did you know that the American ambassador has a pig's head? the Egyptian ambassador would have glanced around cautiously to see if anyone else was listening and then he would have replied: No, that's not possible. This could have been interpreted as an invitation to continue the conversation, which would have been vague, with many twists and turns, because each of them had to make sure he was not subject to some sort of provocation by the other.

Naturally, Armand has not, as of today, had this sort of conversation with the Egyptian ambassador, but it would not be unthinkable. He could have said the part about the pig's head to the Egyptian ambassador, but with the mutually accepted, though unvoiced, assumption that Armand was using it as a bad joke in an attempt to win favor with the Egyptian across the actual boundary lines that apply in the world arena. With this obvious indiscretion on Armand's part, using what would be regarded as a bad joke, he'd be trying, as the Egyptian ambassador had to assume, to win his confidence, no doubt for another purpose than merely passing on a highly inappropriate joke. Yet it's possible that the Egyptian, his interest piqued by all these vague and elaborate references to the American ambassador's animallike appearance and image, might finally allow himself to be carried away by the intriguing and illicit content of these words about the specific pig's head issuing from the mouth of the diplomat from the far North, so that he himself, in the end, might make a reference to his own Arabic knowledge, stubbornly denying that he'd ever heard or thought that the appearance of the American ambassador might remind anyone of, or resemble, a pig's head, even in the artificial lighting of a men's room, while at the same time brusquely admitting that he, in a roundabout way, had become aware of a rumor that in other parts of the world there was *at least* one American diplomat who actually was possessed of what was basically a pig's head atop his muscular body, but that was probably just a malicious rumor, the Egyptian diplomat would have said, and then immediately taken his leave. This sort of conversation, even though in this instance it was only imagined, would indeed have been possible under certain conditions.

But that was not the case when Armand spoke with ambassadors from friendly nations within the European culture. In general, it was unthinkable for him to say to the German, the Dutch, not to mention the Polish ambassador: Did you know that the American ambassador has a pig's head? To say it to the Egyptian ambassador, possibly an honorable man from the third world, was dangerous for both Armand and the Egyptian, but to say it to the friendly Polish ambassador was unthinkable.

These kinds of thoughts, which now raced through Armand's mind as he stood on the terrace facing the illuminated English park and smoked a cigarette while taking a moment to compose himself, did indeed show the realities to which Armand had to relate. What he'd allowed himself to think he'd observed in the men's room was of such a nature that it made him a traitor to Norwegian interests vis-à-vis the United States, and it upset the revered friendliness that Norway had achieved with regard to the most powerful nation in the world. You can think what you like about Norway's close relationship with the United States, but that was the reality with which Armand had to abide. For Armand there were no other options. He could not go over to those who were foreign—not even to get involved in the innocent maligning of envoys from Washington—to representatives of regimes from the third world whose actual legitimacy is based on having the blessing of the United States while they are afraid of their own people. Because this was no innocent maligning. This was no joke. The American ambassador had grasped the point and it would not happen again.

No, it would not happen again. There's no doubt that the West (under the uncontested leadership of the United States) had subjugated the rest of the world, and that we therefore were privileged, that we as a whole (the United States and the close friends of the United States) were the rulers of the world. Then why be so strongly against it? When you're a diplomat, even an ambassador, for a small country that has truly benefited from this? What the hell is your problem, Armand V., thought Armand as he stood there smoking his second cigarette on that mild English autumn evening. Ideas of your youth?

Yet he was against it. And he could do nothing about it. Because he couldn't give it up. Because he was tied to this society and therefore also to its privileged place in relation to power itself, the center of the world; even though that's not really what he wanted. It wasn't the fact that the United States strove for world supremacy that its government, de facto, already had and would rather collapse than lose it; that would have been bearable, something he could bluntly conclude and eventually comment on, in a veiled manner; but the fact that he couldn't let go of being part of the process, that truly shook him. He was an inextricable part of the fabric of power, on its way toward collapse. From such a perspective, which now became shockingly clear to him, he could not hand in his resignation as ambassador. He just couldn't, that was his only and natural response. He had nowhere to go. He was an inextricable part, and all he could do was acknowledge how terrified he was at what he had become inextricably part of. He found himself within the system (as a representative for a small and insignificant country, but at a high diplomatic level) that actually was aiming for world supremacy. And if it did not attain world supremacy, it might as well collapse, as had happened with great empires before.

At a certain point in this lengthy series of arguments that Armand felt compelled to undertake, something merciless came into view. The realization that it had to do with us against them. Who "they" were might vary, just as the "we" might change at different times, but those who are "we" were all inextricable parts, and that included Armand. Armand was an inextricable part; even before he began this lengthy and elaborate argumentation, he had realized it. And at the very end of this endless series of arguments, there was something horrifying that he could not get past, because it was here everything ended. You couldn't get past it, that's what Armand now realized. This end was an elementary requirement, which when spoken of out of turn wasn't so dangerous and could then be tolerated, but when it wasn't spoken about out of turn, it's impossible to get past it. The final requirement that is at the bottom of everything and binds us together is this vow. A requirement, when it is required, to close ranks around the slogan "us vs. them." Armand had gradually come to understand this, in all its horror. And he remained at his job.

"My poor son," he thought as he felt the rush of history seize hold of him, piercing his empty, insignificant individuality, filling it up. Faced with Being and Nothingness. A farm wife's worn-out shoe. A son's failed optic nerve. In spite of everything, Armand thought, I have to confess that I am paralyzed. I can't move, I am paralyzed. I have to confess that I can't avoid it, I really can't.

———

97. It occurs to me that in a previous footnote, long ago, it says that this book takes place in Oslo, abroad, up in the mountains,

and during a sea voyage. Now I merely have to state: there is no sea voyage in this book.

––––––––––

98. Late in the fall, when he came to Oslo for a short visit to conduct consultations on official business, Armand also took a few days off to spend time up in the mountains, and there he met the twin sister, who was standing on the stairs when he arrived at her B and B. It was during the period when October became November, and he was the only guest. The hunters had long since gone home, so there were no more reverberating gunshots to be heard. Nature was quiet except for its own sounds. Both on the first evening and on the two following, he sat in front of the fireplace in the living room of the B and B, talking with the twin sister. It was as if he'd come home, home to this woman who now ran a B and B and who was in the process of closing up the place for the season. He and the twin sister were conversing in subdued and intimate tones. She asked him how he was doing, and he told her that he was doing well, considering the circumstances. She didn't ask him how his son was doing, maybe she was waiting for Armand to bring up the subject, but since Armand did not, she didn't ask. For his part, Armand didn't ask about her husband, from whom she'd separated a few months back, nor how she felt about that happening, and since the twin sister didn't say anything about it, he didn't find out anything regarding where the husband was now or what had caused the breakup in their long-lasting relationship. She had been over forty-five when she got together with this man, who had moved into her B and B up in the mountains and who had also spent the winter months with her in her

spacious apartment in Oslo. Armand's contact with the twin sister had not diminished after she met this man, who was her own age and about the same age as Armand. Nothing had changed between them. They continued their intimate relationship as before. Armand had no problem relating to the twin sister and this husband of hers, whom he liked, although the man was of no real importance to him beyond the fact that he was the man with whom the twin sister lived and with whom she evidently got along well, until she, or he, no longer got along well with him, or her, and he had to leave. When the breakup occurred, the twin sister mentioned it to Armand the next time he came to visit (this was during the summer), and Armand told her he was sorry to hear it, because, as already mentioned, he liked the twin sister's husband. But when the twin sister didn't mention it again, Armand didn't ask about him; after all, it was the twin sister to whom he was connected, to her intimacy and her approval. Thanks to her, he had not lost contact with his own daughter, whom he'd conceived with the twin sister's twin sister. When she had acquired this B and B, she'd taken care of the daughter up here in the summertime, and she'd sent word to Armand, who immediately came to visit if he happened to be in Norway and was able to do so. In this manner he had caught a glimpse of his own daughter for a few days each year as she grew up. And this had led to him attending his daughter's wedding and visiting the couple in their married-student apartment in Bergen later on, and to anticipating the continuation of his family, which had not yet occurred. Now they were sitting in front of the fireplace in the living room of the B and B, having an intimate conversation. He said that in addition to doing well, considering the circumstances, he was also feeling apprehensive, which had led to bad dreams. He was thinking about the world, both the external and internal ones. He said no more than that, and they both fell into an intimate silence, interrupted only by the other person quietly offering a few conciliatory remarks. That was how they spent the first two evenings of his visit to the twin sister's B and B up in the mountains. He had a few pangs of guilty conscience because he'd left his son back at the institute outside London over the weekend to take these extra days in the mountains and visit the twin sister, but he shook off these feelings. There was no use thinking about that. His son had to learn to live his own life, a lonely life, alone with the fact that when he opened his eyes in the morning there was nothing to see, and that wouldn't change as the day went on, as all the days passed, until the end. But right now he was here. With this woman, who exists only in these footnotes with little connection to any unwritten novel. Even though she exists only in these lines, the tooth of time has also taken its toll on her, and left its mark. And that has somehow subdued them. They never confided anything to each other. They shared one secret, from years back, during their younger days. She knew all about his second marriage, and while it lasted, they'd had no contact with each other. Once it was over, Armand, not the twin sister, got in contact again. In the following years the twin sister made occasional visits to the embassies where he was ambassador, staying in a guest room in the residence. At that time she also bought this B and B, and Armand would visit her there. Nothing ever went on between them; they both knew that at any moment they could enter into an intimate relationship, but neither of them wanted that. Not now. Not after Armand had had his second marriage, which he may have always regretted, and yet that's what happened. When he later visited her and she rejected him, he never tried to make a play for her, sexually. He never told her about the women he'd known over the years, with whom he'd had short or long-term relationships; this was over a period of twenty years, from the time of his marriage to his son's mother up until now, and he avoided even mentioning the name of any woman he may have escorted to a specific place or event, maybe not wanting to hurt her, at least that's what he sometimes thought, but he knew it wasn't true. She would not have been hurt; on the other hand, Armand feared that she might have become closed off, or more guarded; in any case a woman's name would cast a shadow over, or get in the way of, the intimacy they both felt characterized their relationship, and then this intimate relationship, merely because of some random name, might come to an end forever. That may seem strange, but I, as the person writing this, think that's the way it was. In spite of the fact that they avoided talking about what most affected them personally, about what was most heartbreaking to them as individuals, and despite the fact that—unless one person insisted, and that happened rarely—they treated each other as tactfully as possible in order to retain what they both would probably call the intimacy of their relationship, Armand would still maintain that he could talk to her about everything. They carried on intimate conversations, he listened to her, she listened to him. She was the one who could offer him approval. This relationship, which had lasted thirty years and was linked to a tacit agreement, a secret that excluded so much and made it impossible for them to talk to each other about everything, can be viewed as a distillate illustrating the melancholy which this special, disconnected, but possibly satellite-like footnote expresses.

He stayed up in the mountains for three days. In the daytime he took long hikes over the slopes. It was late in the fall, as October merged into November. The B and B would soon close for the season, and the twin sister was busy packing up and stowing away everything, so she couldn't go with him on these long hikes. The hunters had long since gone home, so there were no more reverberating gunshots to be heard. Nature was quiet except for its own sounds: the rain pouring down; the fog, which sounded damp; the wind blowing against the B and B's wooden siding, which creaked; the tiny crackling of brittle ice that showed up wherever there was a trace of water, from the big expanses of water on ponds and lakes, to the moisture on the trampled grass and moss, and on the steep, rough trails; the mighty presence of the mountain peaks in poor visibility, like a peal of thunder. Armand went on long hikes, taking in deep breaths of the soothing mountain air. On the third day he said goodbye to the twin sister and drove his rental car back to Oslo. From there, he would return to London.

98 B. "Nature was quiet except for its own sounds." That's what it says, and I have to accept it, though not without this footnote. Nature is, of course, a neuter noun, but not in Norwegian. So out of respect for the structures of Norwegian grammar, and given Armand's low sense of national identity, I have to submit.

99. After this short visit to the mountains, Armand arrived in Oslo and turned in his rental car. Then he took public transportation to a station near his son's rented room and headed for the apartment building. He had sublet his own apartment after the Misfortune occurred, when he realized he needed all the money he could scrape together in order to give his son the best opportunities. He did this so he wouldn't have to fight with foot-dragging bureaucrats in the defense and social services ministries or comparable functionaries in the private and public insurance companies for his son to receive the compensation to which he was entitled; instead, he could take his time getting help and calmly await the payments in the future. Yet he had continued to pay his son's rent to the malicious widow in the confused hope that his son might still fully recover and regain his eyesight, even though he'd been told explicitly this would never happen. He had gone to see the old widow and paid the rent for a year, assuring her that his son would still need the room, a room of his own, whether he stayed in the military or began to study; and now he was on his way over there to stay the night before he caught the plane back to London the next morning. Of course he could have stayed somewhere else, in a hotel or with someone he knew, he could have even stayed at the twin sister's place, as she was still at the B and B up in the mountains about to close up for the season—her spacious apartment was empty and he could have easily borrowed it—but he preferred to go to his son's room, which he had paid for after all. He walked up Kirkeveien, heading for his son's locked and unused room. He was wearing his vacation attire, his mountain clothes,

and he carried a suitcase that contained, among other things, suits, pressed shirts, ties, etc. It was late in the evening, because he'd gone to a simple restaurant, where he'd sat for a long time eating dinner and drinking wine before he took the subway to the Majorstua station. He used the key to let himself in, first the front door of the building, then the door to the dark apartment, and then he unlocked the door to his son's room. He switched on the light and found himself standing in the middle of the room, which had remained untouched until now. He opened the window, found some linens in the cupboard, and made up the bed. Then he went straight to sleep. He had set the alarm clock for seven because the plane left early in the morning. He woke up when it rang, got out of bed, and washed in the small sink in the room. Then he crept out to the toilet and took care of business as quietly as he could, though he couldn't avoid flushing when he was done. Back to the room. He got dressed. Put on a shirt, tie, and one of the suits he'd brought along. Then he looked at himself in the mirror. He packed his suitcase, putting in his mountain clothing, which was a tight fit, but the clothes didn't make it too heavy. He made the bed. He heard sounds coming from the kitchen. He put on his coat and his elegant cashmere scarf. He stood still for a moment because he dreaded making an appearance in the doorway now that sounds were coming from the kitchen. But he opened the door and stepped into the kitchen. The young student was sitting at the table drinking coffee. Armand told him that he'd spent the night in Are's room.

"So how is Are doing?" asked the student.

"Good," replied the father, "really good."

"Is he coming back?" asked the student.

"I think he'll be studying in England," said the father.

"So he won't be coming here anymore?"

"Probably not, but the room is paid for until April of next year. So, we'll have to wait and see."

At that moment the widow came into the kitchen. She gave Armand a suspicious look but sat down at the table across from the young student. She poured herself some coffee. She took a slice of bread that the student evidently had cut from the loaf and smeared on a thick layer of butter as she stared with her ancient and intense eyes at Norway's ambassador to London. She was about to say something, but the young student spoke first, asking: "Would you like a cup of coffee?"

"No," replied Armand, "I've got to go. I have to catch a plane." He headed for the door. He was waiting for the widow to call after him. To say he owed her more money. That his son hadn't paid for something or other. But that didn't happen.

"Goodbye," he said and opened the apartment door.

They nodded in reply.

"Well, you're entitled to it," said the widow. "I can't deny you that."

"What do you mean?"

"Spending the night here. But I'm going to send you a letter canceling the rental agreement when the time you've paid for is up."